DADDY'S LITTLE CUPCAKE

MISSOURI DADDIES
BOOK ONE

EVERLY RAINE

CONTENTS

Cover artist: Scott Carpenter

Editor: Sara Guthman at Foxtale Editing

To everyone who helped me along this journey of self publishing my book

BLURB

Charlotte is shy and insecure. With her life working at the bakery, she's had to suppress her little side to make ends meet. But all she wishes for is for someone to be her Daddy. And even when she does find one, she feels that he doesn't want her, in any shape or form.

Finn is a Daddy Dom. He's one of the owners of a club, specifically BTK. But whenever he finds a potential little, they are all fake toward him. When he almost throws in the towel and gives up on finding his little girl, his gaze finds her. She's coloring on the floor in his club, and immediately after speaking with her, he knows she's going to be his.

Charlotte wasn't sure of Finn, and she still isn't. Yet Finn is going to prove to her that she is meant to be Daddy's Little Cupcake.

DADDY'S LITTLE CUPCAKE

MISSOURI DADDIES

Book One

CONTENT WARNINGS

This is an age play book. If you are comfortable reading about the things listed below then this is the book for you!

- age play
-ABDL
-spicy scenes
-discipline (including spanking, corner time, and more)

CHAPTER ONE

CHARLOTTE

"*D*iana is here!" James told Charlotte as he walked into the kitchen. "Turn the oven off, and you can leave."

Charlotte turned the oven off, grabbed her things, and headed out of the bakery and into her friend's car. Today was one of the days her friend picked her up and dropped her off at her house.

Diana didn't always pick her up because she had work, but when she did, Charlotte was thankful. The walk wasn't long to her house, but after a day full of baking delicious treats, it was nice to be off her feet.

"Buckle up," Diana reminded Charlotte as she slipped into the car.

She had a tendency to forget to buckle herself up. Charlotte wasn't in cars a lot; she didn't like to drive, and Diana didn't pick her up a lot.

"Good girl, Charlie. Now, how was work today?" Diana asked as she pulled out of the driveway.

Charlotte loved and hated when Diana called her Charlie. When she was in little space, that's what Diana called her. It always made her feel small and ready to just be little.

"It was fine," Charlotte whispered.

It was anything but fine. The past hour had been an absolute wreck, and Charlotte didn't want to tell Diana about it. She knew she would get an earful about it from her, about her safety and all, and she already got that from James, her boss who was also a Daddy Dom to his wife who worked with her.

Charlotte shuddered at the thought of what happened an hour ago. She was taking out cupcakes from the oven when she stepped on a towel that was hanging from the oven's handle and slipped. It was like it happened just a couple of minutes ago, still fresh on her mind.

Charlotte placed all of her weight on her feet as she lifted the heavy and hot cupcake pan out of the oven. She let out a high pitched squeal as her foot slipped from under her, the cupcake pan flying out of her hands and landing on the ground with a loud bang, as cupcake crumbles flew everywhere in the kitchen.

She landed hard on her bottom, a small scream came out of her mouth, and her hand reached around to rub her abused bottom.

"Owie." Her butt was throbbing.

Wincing, she pulled herself off the ground and looked around. Horror filled her face as she took in the state of the kitchen. Pieces of cupcake littered the whole kitchen floor.

Tears sprang to Charlotte's eyes as an overwhelming feeling flowed through her body. All that hard work had gone down the drain in a couple of seconds. What was she going to do with such limited time to make more cupcakes? There was

3

almost no chance they'd cool enough to frost before the customer arrived.

"Charlotte?" Diana called out her name. "Are you paying attention to me?"

She still felt the fear, adrenaline, and worry that coursed through her body. The worry that she wouldn't be able to get the cupcakes out to the customer and disappoint James at the same time.

Mishaps had been happening at the bakery more and more recently. She didn't intend for them, and she always managed to fix the problem, but James found out about each and every one of them and hadn't fired her yet. Charlotte worried that each time she made a mistake, he would fire her, but he never did and kept telling her that he wouldn't.

Turning her head, she looked over at Diana before she looked out the window and didn't recognize the surroundings.

"Where are we going?" Charlotte asked.

"That's what I was trying to tell you. We're going to BTS tonight. You remember Behind the Scenes, the club for littles, Daddies, and Mommies?" Diana said, briefly glancing at Charlotte.

Fear coursed through Charlotte's body. She didn't want to go to BTS.

"Anywhere but there," she found herself saying.

BTS was a BDSM club that a lot of people went to. It really catered to littles and their caregivers, but they had smaller sections for other aspects of BDSM.

"I think it'll be great for you to go. I know you've been suppressing your little side more. It'll be good for you to go and let go. Maybe you'll find a Daddy of your own." Diana drove to the club.

Charlotte shook her head. As much as she wanted a Daddy, she didn't want to look for one right now. She was exhausted and wanted to sleep; she didn't want to go out and play. That's what she told herself anyway. Deep down, she knew that she wanted to let her little free. She didn't want to be held back anymore.

She was stressed from life, not having enough money to pay bills, and working a lot. Charlotte had a problem when she was little; she loved to buy things she saw on TV commercials or the internet: stuffies, baby bottles, blankies, and pacifiers.

Recently, she'd woken after spending a night in little space to find her computer littered with open internet tabs. After feverishly clicking through them—tallying each purchase as she went—Charlotte had discovered she'd spent over two hundred dollars on things she didn't need and couldn't afford.

She tried to cancel the order and return them, but they wouldn't allow her to cancel, and the return label would have cost more for each package than the stuff was worth. That's when she realized she couldn't be in little space unsupervised. The problem was Charlotte didn't have anyone to supervise her.

Diana was a Mommy, but she wasn't Charlotte's Mommy. Besides, if Diana were to see Charlotte's home right then, Charlotte might die of embarrassment. It was a complete mess. Her little was *not* very organized.

She didn't have a Daddy to take care of her, keep her on track, discipline her when she did something naughty, and cherish her when she succeeded at something out of her comfort zone.

That was part of the reason why Charlotte didn't want to go to the club. It showed what she didn't have right now and what she couldn't have. Since she had been suppressing her little, each time she slipped, it was harder and harder to get pulled out of it.

"We're staying there for at least thirty minutes. If you really don't want to be there after that, we'll leave. But I think this will do great things," Diana said as she pulled into the parking spot.

Charlotte groaned. Thirty minutes was a long time, and she didn't know how she was going to survive that time. What if she slipped into little space for the whole thirty minutes and couldn't pull out?

How was she going to take care of herself when she got home? There were so many questions that ran through her head, and she didn't know the answer to them. Diana wouldn't come home and spend the night with her, not that Charlotte would allow her to.

She hadn't been in her house, and Charlotte wasn't going to let her come in. It was a mess, and Diana would be disappointed in the state of it.

"Ready?" Diana asked.

Nodding her head, Charlotte climbed out of the car and grabbed Diana's hand as they walked toward the club front doors.

CHAPTER TWO

FINN

*F*inn thought tonight was going to be like every other night. Come to work, watch people, walk around to make sure everything was running smoothly, go home, and crash for the night.

It was exhausting doing this every night, but he had to. Well, he didn't *have* to because there were eight other club owners. Finn didn't have to be here every night, he chose to be here.

He worked well over the normal forty hours per week, but he didn't have anything better to do. He didn't have anyone to come home to or many friends or family that were outside of the other eight owners. It was just a cold, dark, life-less house, and he avoided going there unless he had to sleep.

Sometimes Finn found himself sleeping in his office so he didn't have to go home. It was better to be in a club that had people in it, feeling like he wasn't alone, than to go home and be alone. He thought about going home early tonight to get some good sleep, but something stopped him. Or, well, someone stopped him.

Finn was walking by the window that faced the club's big playroom. His eyes were immediately drawn to the little girl that walked in through the entrance. She was absolutely breathtaking with her long red hair and green eyes. She looked tense, and it took everything in him not to stalk downstairs and ask her what was wrong.

He didn't like when the littles that came into the club were tense. He wanted everyone to be comfortable and let go while they were here. That was why all nine of them came up with the club, so people like them could have a safe place to come to.

He wanted anyone to come in and be safe, *feel* safe, and most cases that happened, but there were a few who came in and didn't feel that way. One of the nine owners always listened and tried to make them more comfortable.

That was what Finn wanted to do right now. He wanted to go to the girl and ask how he could make her more comfortable. Ask why she was so tense and see if he could help any, but this wasn't like all the other times. He felt a connection toward her, and he couldn't explain it.

He had seen her walk in with a lady, probably her Mommy since she wasn't doing anything. Finn's heart broke with that thought.

He didn't know why he was feeling this way toward this particular little. Finn also had never taken an interest in any little since opening the club several years ago with his friends. He had never seen her before.

How had he never seen her before? Could she have come whenever he wasn't in the club or in meetings and couldn't look at the guests?

He didn't like to mix work with pleasure, but how else

was he going to find that special girl for him? It was hard to go outside of the club and meet people. He had tried it before, but the person just wanted to be with him and faked being little.

He knew it wasn't all like, that but he couldn't help not wanting to do it anymore because of that one instance.

It was also hard for Finn to find a little. Once a little heard that he was one of the owners, they changed. They tried to impress him and make Finn like them more. They acted fake, and he didn't like that. He didn't want that either. He wanted a genuine little who didn't have to act a certain way.

It never worked. Once they changed, Finn knew what they were like. He hated judging people, but he also didn't want to waste his time. He was getting older, and all he wanted to do was settle down with his little girl and live his life.

Finn was also a very busy man, as he worked long hours for the club. All of his friends and co-owners wanted him to take more time off and try to find a little. They could see how stressed he was.

Finn scoffed at that several times. None of the other owners had littles of their own. They were all searching for a little to cherish. Finn thought that they needed to focus on finding their own and not worrying about him and his life.

He thought back to the little girl that was downstairs. She was different. He didn't know how, maybe how she acted, but she was different.

And Finn was intrigued.

He watched the little move over to the coloring corner and pick out a book and markers. She was absolutely precious, lying on her stomach, her legs kicking every once in a while.

The woman she came with walked over and placed a sippy cup and some crackers beside her.

Who was this woman?

Was she the little's Mommy?

Finn watched the lady as she went back to her seat. She watched the little girl for a bit before her eyes started to wander. She was looking over at two boys who were playing with the toy cars together. Finn could see a longing in her eyes because he too felt like that.

They both just wanted someone to cherish.

Realization hit Finn. The lady wasn't the girl's Mommy. She was probably a friend who brought her here.

A smile tugged on his face. If the little girl had a Daddy, he would have come with her.

Finn was going to try his luck and talk to her. The worst she could say was that she already had a Daddy and that he wasn't there. He felt a pull to her, and he didn't want to ignore it.

This was the first time in years he felt a pull toward someone, and he wasn't about to let it go down the drain.

Finn's friend, Mac, and also one of the other owners walked up next to him.

"You've been staring at her for a while. Going to go talk to her?" Mac asked. "If you don't, I think I might. She's super cute with her feet moving back and forth as she colors. I don't think she'll mind me coming and talking to her."

Finn growled and looked over at Mac. "Back off."

Mac laughed and patted his shoulder. Finn knew right then and there that Mac was playing with him and wanted to get a reaction. He should have known better than to fall into that trap.

He was normally good at seeing right through Mac and his games, but this time he didn't. He was too engrossed as he watched the little color that he didn't look at all the cues he was giving him, and Mac knew.

"Well, go talk to her. Who knows, by the time you get down there, she could be gone," Mac said and walked away.

Finn stood up from his chair and made his way toward the front door. His office, well, the lounge area that everyone sat in while people played was on the second floor and looked over the whole club. It was a huge room.

"Where are you going?" Marco asked right before Finn could exit the room.

Marco was another one of the other owners who liked to hang around people. He didn't have to be doing anything, but he preferred not to be alone. Maybe that's why Finn and Marco got along so well. They were both lonely and just wanted to be around people.

"Downstairs," Finn replied and walked out of the room.

He didn't want to explain to his friends and co-owners what he was going to do. He knew that they would be looking out the window and watching him. Finn rarely went down-stairs when the club was open. He didn't want people coming up to him and trying to be his friend.

Most people at the club only wanted to be his friend so they could ask for discounts. Well, it was mostly girls that did. There was the occasional male sub that would ask, but that was rare.

Finn quickly made his way down the stairs and toward the little room. He didn't want to take a long time and find out the little girl left. That would make Finn sad and feel like he missed out on something.

He opened the door and looked over at the coloring corner. His whole body relaxed at the sight of the little girl still coloring. He hadn't missed her.

CHAPTER THREE

CHARLOTTE

*C*harlotte had been lying on her stomach for the past five minutes, coloring. She hadn't been able to fall into little space, and she had a suspicion why. She was worried about adult things and couldn't seem to let go of it.

Every scenario ran through her head on how she could get herself out of this problem, but each one was talking to someone and explaining her situation. Something she didn't want to do because then people would know her situation.

Maybe it was time for her to go back to Diana and tell her that it was time for them to leave. She didn't want to be here the whole time and not be comfortable and be little.

Right as Charlotte was about to get up, she heard footsteps near her.

"Hello, little one," a man said softly to her.

FINN

Finn spoke softly to the little girl in front of him. He didn't want to spook her by talking in his normal voice.

His deep voice tended to scare little girls at first. Finn was always mindful when it came to littles and tried not to scare them. He knew that a lot of them were scared of strange people, especially strange, tall people. Finn was tall, and in the beginning, he didn't care if he scared littles because it just meant they stayed away from him.

Well, the genuine ones did. The ones that wanted to sink their claws into him because he was one of the owners didn't care one bit that he was taller and his voice was deeper. That was another thing he looked for but not a defining one that made him walk away from the little.

Some littles really didn't mind the deep voice or a tall stranger coming near them, and he had to remember that.

"Hello, sir," the little girl whispered before she looked back down at her coloring book.

"What are you coloring?" Finn found himself asking.

He was drawn to this little girl, and he didn't want to leave her.

"A cupcake." The little girl's voice went higher. She giggled and continued to color the frosting a red color. "A Christmas cupcake."

"Is Christmas your favorite holiday?" Finn sat down on the ground next to her and watched her color in the lines.

He wondered if she always colored in the lines or if she colored outside sometimes. It was pretty normal for littles to color outside of the lines, well, younger littles. Finn was curious to see what age this little girl would fall into.

She looked up at Finn and nodded her head rapidly. "Yes!" she squealed.

Finn watched the girl as she went back to coloring, but this time she was coloring something new. A piece of cake. He wondered if this little girl had a sweet tooth that he would have to watch out for. He didn't want his baby girl to get sick from all the sweets.

His body froze at that thought. Shit. He just called her his baby girl. He doesn't even know her name, and he was already claiming her.

"What's your name, little one?" Finn asked.

"Charlie," she said as she colored the piece of cake blue. "Charlotte is my full name." Her voice was more grown up this time.

Finn knew that she probably preferred to be called Charlie when she was in little space and Charlotte when she wasn't. He wanted to come up with a nickname that would be meaningful if they ever got serious. He hoped that they would. She seemed so shy, but he felt like she wouldn't be when she got more comfortable around him.

Now to figure out how to get her comfortable around him so they could get to know each other better.

"My name's Finn," he said, hoping she would look at him again.

She had only looked at him once this whole time, and he wanted her to look up again. He wanted to see her pretty eyes and face.

"Can I color with you?" Finn asked.

A shocked look fell on the girl's face, and Finn wondered why. Had no one else ever asked Charlotte if they could color with her?

"It's okay if you don't want me to color with you. I just want to get to know you, and I do love coloring," Finn said, gaining her attention again.

Charlotte shyly looked at his chest, and Finn felt like she was hesitant on what to do.

"Well, I don't want to make you uncomfortable. It was nice meeting you," he said, his tone of voice holding a note of disappointment and sadness.

"Wait!" Charlotte said, panic clear in her voice. "Y-you can s-stay and color if you want," she whispered.

Finn smiled and sat down next to her. "Can you tear a picture out for me so I can color with you?"

Her eyes went wide as she looked at Finn. "You can't tear it out! It's not mine, it's the club's," she whispered.

"It's okay. I give you permission," Finn said, giving her an encouraging smile.

Charlotte shook her head and looked at the coloring book. What was going on inside of her head right now? He thought it might have been because she didn't want to get into trouble. Well, she wouldn't, but she didn't know that. She probably didn't even know who he was.

"I'm one of the owners of the club. It's okay to tear a picture out for me," he explained.

She didn't move, so Finn picked up the coloring book from her and tore a picture out before placing the book back in front of her again.

"There, now if one of my friends comes and says some-thing, I'll get in trouble and you won't," Finn said.

Charlotte giggled.

"What are you giggling about?" he asked.

"Nofing," she mumbled, sobering up quickly.

Finn let out a sigh. Baby steps. She obviously wasn't comfortable around him yet, but he was going to change that.

"I used to color when I was a kid. I haven't in years, too much work," Finn said as he started to color the ice cream cone.

Out of the corner of his eye, he saw Charlotte start to color her piece of cake again, adding blue and pink to the picture. Her forehead creased like she was thinking about something really hard, and Finn wanted to know.

"What are you thinking so hard about?" He sat down his marker and looked at her fully.

"What flavor this would be in real life or if it would just be dyed," Charlotte said, her voice going higher.

Finn couldn't help but smile when he heard that. She was getting more comfortable around him and slowly slipping into little space.

"Would it be strawberry flavored?" he asked.

"I've made a strawberry flavored cake before, and it was delicious," she said, getting excited.

"With what type of frosting?"

"Chocolate!" she giggled. "There's no other flavor that it can go with."

Finn chuckled. "I agree."

Charlotte nodded her head and went back to coloring. He took this time to watch her as she colored and let go some, but that quickly ended when she groaned and put her head down on the coloring book.

"What's wrong?" Finn asked, rubbing his hand up and down her back.

Her body stiffened with the contact but quickly melted under his touch as he continued to soothe her.

"Can you look at me, little cupcake?" Finn asked gently.

Charlotte shook her head.

"Please, my little cupcake," he encouraged her.

He knew it probably wasn't the wisest idea to call her his little cupcake since she wasn't his, but right now, he didn't care. He wanted to know what was wrong.

Charlotte slowly lifted her head up and looked at Finn's mouth. He had seen several littles do this when they were nervous or intimidated.

"Look me in the eyes," he commanded.

Her eyes immediately found his.

"Good girl," he said, praising her.

She blushed but continued to look in his eyes. Such a good girl following orders and not looking away, even though she probably wanted to.

"Now, can you tell me what's wrong?" he asked. He posed it as a question, but the tone of his voice had an edge to it that made it seem more like a command.

"I d-don't want to scare you off," she mumbled.

"You won't scare me off. Now you can tell me."

She took a deep breath in. "I just want to let go." She looked down at her hands.

"So let go," Finn encouraged her. "I'll watch over you."

Charlotte shook her head.

"Why not?" he asked, trying to figure out why she wouldn't want to let go. When it was apparent that she wasn't going to answer, Finn spoke again. "You can tell me anything." He ran his hand up and down her back.

She looked at him, tears in her eyes. "I don't want to mess up," she sobbed out.

"Oh, honey," Finn said, moving his hand off of her back. "Come here." His arms opened wide for her.

Charlotte moved quickly into his arms, her legs on either side of his body. He slowly started to rock them back and forth, trying to calm her down.

"Everything's going to be okay. You won't mess up," he whispered in her ear as he ran a hand up and down her back.

Finn pulled back to get a better look at Charlotte's face.

"Why do you think you're going to mess up?" he asked, wiping away the tears on her face.

"I d-don't know," she stuttered out.

"I think you do," he said with a smile on his face. He gave her nose a little tap. "You can tell me."

"I've never had a Daddy before, and I don't want to mess up the chance of getting one," she mumbled and looked down at her hands.

His heart broke but warmed at the same time. It broke because she was so scared of doing something wrong and messing it all up, but his heart warmed because she thought of him as maybe her potential Daddy.

"Charlie, can you look at me?" Finn asked softly.

Charlotte looked up at Finn, and his hand cupped her cheek.

"You won't disappoint me because you haven't had a Daddy yet. If anything, that makes you special in your own way," he said and kissed her forehead.

Finn saw her close her eyes as tears started to well up in them.

"How about you let go and be little, if you're comfortable, and I'll watch over you. We can go over rules and your safe word first," he suggested.

19

She nodded her head.

"Great! Now, what's your safe word?" he asked. Finn was running his hands through her hair now, and from the look on her face, he knew she loved it.

"Red," she said. "It's easy to remember because I tend to forget things."

"Good girl," Finn mumbled and gave her a smile. "What are your hard limits?"

"No humiliation. No cane. No drawing blood or degrading me," Charlotte confidently replied.

"Good. I don't like those either," he said. "What about punishments? Are spankings, corner time, paddle, lines, edging okay?"

Finn let Charlotte think about it for a second.

"No." She shook her head.

"No, they are a hard limit, or no, they are okay?" Finn asked.

Charlotte blushed and looked down at her hands.

"No, they are okay," she whispered.

Finn placed his fingers under her chin and lifted her head. "Don't be embarrassed. There's nothing wrong. I just wanted to clarify and not assume anything."

Charlotte nodded and continued to look at him. When Finn first started to train to become a Dom, he had assumed some things and almost hurt the sub. Thankfully, it was in a class, so the sub knew, and there were other Doms in the room that were watching over, so nothing happened.

"Now, do you want to discuss anything else, or would you like to go back to coloring?" Finn ran his fingers through her hair again.

"Color," Charlotte said and relaxed in his arms.

"Can you color me a picture? I would love to take it home and hang it up on my fridge."

"Yes," she whispered.

Finn picked Charlotte up and placed her back down on the ground where she was before. She got comfortable and picked up her pink marker, and he couldn't bring himself to look away from her.

"Charlotte, it's time to go," Diana, her friend, said.

"No," Charlotte said.

CHAPTER FOUR

CHARLOTTE

*C*harlotte didn't want to leave yet. She wanted to color a picture for Finn. Couldn't Diana see that? Why did she have to come right this instant when things were just getting good. Diana knew better than that.

"Charlotte," Diana's voice warned her.

She ignored Diana, though, and started to color the cupcake.

"Little one, you are being rude to your friend. There are consequences for being rude and not doing as you're told. Do you want a spanking?" Finn asked.

Charlotte looked up at Finn with wide eyes. Crap. She didn't want a spanking, but she wanted to finish the picture for him. With that thought in her mind, she went back to coloring the cupcake.

A big hand grabbed her around the waist and picked her up. She screamed when Diana grabbed the marker from her hand.

"No!" she yelled. Charlotte tried to get out of Finn's

embrace, but his arms just tightened around her. "Let me go!"

"Naughty little girls get spankings," Finn said. He stood up and walked them over to a big chair.

Charlotte gulped when she realized it was the spanking chair. The spanking chair that no little wanted to go to. It was out in the public room, meaning when a little gets spanked, every other little watched. Every Mommy and Daddy watched as the person got spanked.

It was mortifying, but at the same time, it was exhilarating. Charlotte had never gotten spanked before at the club. She never stepped out of line, but she was also not here very often.

Charlotte was mortified that she made a scene in the club. She'd never acted out before, and she didn't know why she was doing it now.

Could it be that having Finn around was making her do this? She didn't want to leave him?

"Please no," Charlotte begged Finn as he sat down on the chair.

"You were a naughty girl. Naughty girls get punished," Finn said.

"I'll be a good girl." Charlotte raised her voice.

She struggled in Finn's arms as he put her over his lap. So many emotions were going through Charlotte as she laid there. Did she really just act out? Was she really getting her first punishment at the club?

Charlotte stilled in Finn's lap. Finn was one of the owners. The owners of the club. Was he really going to spank her?

"Sir, I can punish her if you want. I'm the one that's

supposed to be looking over her," Diana said. "You don't have to take time from your busy schedule to punish her. We were just about to leave, but I'll punish her when we get home."

Charlotte struggled in Finn's lap. She didn't want to get spanked by him or by Diana. She didn't want to get punished at all, but she knew that saying no to them was a big mistake. Charlotte knew better than to say no to a Mommy or Daddy. Especially when they told her that it was time to go home.

"She was rude to you and ignored me. I will give her the punishment, if that's okay," Finn said, brooking no argument.

"No!" Charlotte shouted. She didn't want to get punished. She didn't deserve a punishment, but deep down, she knew she needed this.

Charlotte also knew that he could punish her if he wanted. She signed the form that if any unattended little disobeyed or was naughty, they could get punished by a Daddy in the club. Not just any Daddy, but one of the staff that was a Daddy. The club didn't want just anyone able to give out punishments to unattended littles because they could be a mess.

Charlotte technically wasn't unattended, but Diana nodded to Finn that it was okay.

This club used the light system, so if she needed to get out of a situation, all she had to do was say red, and it would stop. It eased her knowing that, but at the same time, it didn't. She didn't want to get punished.

Finn placed a hand on Charlotte's butt, making a little squeal fall past her lips. His hands were massive, but Charlotte's butt didn't fit in his hand.

"I'm going to spank you now. This first time I'll allow you to have your pants on, but if you disobey again, then your pants and underwear come off," Finn said, slowly moving his palm around Charlotte's butt.

Charlotte wiggled around, trying to get out of this hold, but it didn't work. His right arm was holding Charlotte's back in place while his left hand was on her butt, successfully holding her in place.

"No. Please don't. I'll be a good girl," Charlotte begged.

She really didn't want to get spanked. She had heard all about it, and it kind of scared her.

Charlotte's breathing started to pick up as she thought of this. She'd never had somebody do this before, and she didn't know if she wanted Finn to. She didn't know him that well.

Her chest started to feel restricted as her breathing got faster. Charlotte clawed at Finn's thighs as she tried to get a breath into her lungs.

"Whoa, Charlotte?" Finn asked. "Are you okay?"

Charlotte didn't answer, though. She felt the hands on her body, moving her so that she was sitting up on his lap and not over his lap.

"Look at me," Finn demanded.

Charlotte looked at him, her breathing still really fast. Finn looked behind her, and she could only assume he was looking at her friend, Diana. Was he going to pass Charlotte to her friend?

Hurt flashed through her chest, and she gasped for a breath of air. Charlotte didn't know Finn very well, but he had been so kind to her, and the thought of him passing her back to her friend hurt.

"Charlotte," Finn said, gaining her attention. "I need you to take a deep breath for me."

She looked away from Finn and closed her eyes tight. Charlotte didn't want to see him hand her off.

"Charlotte." Hands gripped her chin and pulled her head back to where it was before. "Look at me."

She didn't look, though. Charlotte couldn't look into Finn's eyes as he told her that he never wanted to see her again. She couldn't take that.

"Look at me now," Finn demanded.

Charlotte opened her eyes and looked at Finn. His face didn't show any hatred but compassion and worry.

"Take a deep breath with me," he said.

She found herself taking in a deep breath, slowly calming down with him.

"That's it. You're doing so well," Finn murmured quietly. "Good girl."

Charlotte's cheeks turned red when he called her a good girl. Not many people had told her that, and it made her feel all gooey inside when Finn said it.

"What happened?" he asked.

Charlotte looked down at her lap, feeling embarrassed. Would Finn make fun of her for never having a punishment before or feeling hurt that she thought he was going to give her back to Diana?

"Charlotte," Finn's voice warned her. "I need to know what happened so I can make it better."

Her heart went all gooey with those words. He wanted to make it all better. Did he care that much for her?

"I'm embarrassed," Charlotte whispered, not looking up at him.

Finn's hand gripped her chin again and lifted her head up.

"Don't be embarrassed. I won't make fun of you," he whispered back.

Charlotte blinked several times, trying to get rid of the tears that started to appear in her eyes.

"I've never been spanked before," Charlotte mumbled, hoping Finn didn't hear a word she said. "I was scared."

"Little one, can you say that again?" he asked.

Charlotte shook her head.

"Little one, please."

Tears sprung into her eyes, and she blinked several times but was unsuccessful when they spilled out of her eyes and down her cheeks.

"Oh, little one, it's going to be okay," Finn said as he wiped away the tears on her cheeks. "That's it. It's okay. Now, can you tell me what you said?"

Charlotte didn't want to tell him, but she knew he wasn't going to let it go until she did. She buried her head into Finn's chest.

"I've never been spanked before," Charlotte whispered, hiding her face in his chest. "I was scared."

She wondered what he thought about that. Would he want nothing to do with her now since she had never been spanked before? Charlotte felt tears appear in her eyes again, ready to spill at any second.

"Little one, it's okay to be scared the first time. It's all new, but it's going to be okay. I'm going to take care of you," Finn said, running his hands up and down Charlotte's back.

Charlotte shook her head, not liking it at all. She didn't want to get spanked.

"You're not getting out of this," Finn said, slightly pulling her back to look at her.

Charlotte whimpered, trying to get back to cover her face. She didn't want him to see her tear-filled eyes again, and she certainly didn't want to get spanked. Maybe if she kept crying, he wouldn't spank her.

"I'm scared," Charlotte finally said when she couldn't get her face back into his chest. "It's going to hurt."

Charlotte felt Finn starting to move a little, and she looked up to see why. He was lightly laughing, which brought more tears to her eyes.

"Of course it's going to hurt," he chuckled. "It's a punishment; it's supposed to hurt. You're supposed to learn from it. Once it's done, all is forgiven, and we move on."

Charlotte shook her head and tried to get out of his lap. He was not going to spank her. She wouldn't allow it. Yes, she did disobey, but all she wanted to do was color him a picture. What was wrong with doing that?

"All I wanted to do was color you a picture." She looked up at him innocently. "I was almost done, so I had to finish it."

"Your friend Diana said it was time to go. She's responsible for you tonight, which means she sets the rules, and you need to pay attention to them. You can't just disobey because you want to color me a picture," Finn said as he rubbed his thumb across Charlotte's cheek. "And then you disobeyed me as well. Those two can't go unpunished, which means you're getting spanked."

Charlotte thrashed around, trying to get out of his embrace. Finn quickly held her up and landed two swats to her butt. She yelled out, not expecting the two spankings she just got.

"Owie," Charlotte whined as she rubbed her butt.

Finn quickly grabbed her hand, stopping her from rubbing her butt. "Naughty girls don't get to rub their butt."

"That hurt," Charlie whimpered.

"They did not. They just took you by surprise, and it scared you a little but those are just warnings. These are actually the real spankings you're about to get," Finn said as he looked directly into her eyes.

Charlotte shook her head but quickly faltered and then nodded her head. It didn't really hurt as much as she'd thought it would, it just scared her like Finn had said.

"Now, are you ready for your punishment?" Finn asked. "Are you going to take it like a good girl?"

Charlotte shook her head. "No, I'm not ready."

Finn laughed and held her cheeks in his hands. "I don't think you're ever going to be ready, but I'm going to take good care of you. Be my good little girl and lay over my lap and take the punishment? All will be forgiven after."

She thought about it for a second. She loved it when he called her little girl, especially when he asked if she was going to be his good little girl. She wanted to be his good little girl, but she'd never had a Daddy before, and she didn't want to mess anything up.

"Charlie?" Finn said, bringing her out of her thoughts.

"O-otay," she whispered as she looked into his eyes.

He said he was going to take good care of her, and she believed him. Finn helped Charlotte off of his lap and got into position, patting his thighs for her to lay over.

Charlotte gulped when she realized that she was about to get punished in front of the whole club. Was she ready for this?

"Charlie? Everything's going to be okay," Finn said, patting his lap again.

Charlie looked up at Finn and stared into his eyes. She doubted herself for a second; she shouldn't be doing this, but she knew that the guilt of disobeying both of them was going to eat her up inside.

Diana had punished her before, but it was either lines or standing in a corner. Diana never spanked her.

Charlotte took a step back, and her eyes went wide when Finn's hand wrapped around her wrist. She had just made yet another mistake, and she was going to pay for it.

CHAPTER FIVE

CHARLOTTE

*H*er heart was racing as Finn lightly tugged her hand, pulling her toward him. She didn't know what to do. Charlotte didn't want to get herself into more trouble, but she couldn't seem to stop.

First talking back to Diana and Finn. Then telling Finn no and trying to get away. And lastly taking a step back when Finn gave her a chance to lay over his lap.

Charlotte was in a lot of trouble, and she knew it.

"I gave you a chance," Finn said, making a *tsk* sound.

Charlotte flinched and hung her head. If she could go back in time and not take a step back, she would. She would go back and make sure she didn't tell Diana and Finn no if it meant not getting spanked.

Now Charlotte had to go through with the punishment.

"Are you going to be a good girl and take your punishment?" Finn asked as he tugged Charlotte closer to him.

She nodded her head and looked at his lap. Charlotte didn't want to see the disappointment in Finn's eyes. She didn't know him that well, but she did know that if she saw it, it was going to break her heart.

"Eyes on me, little cupcake," Finn demanded.

Charlotte shook her head, tears filling her eyes.

"Charlotte." His voice held a warning to it.

She quickly looked up from his lap and into his eyes. Charlotte didn't see any disappointment lingering on his face or in his eyes, and she let out a little breath at that.

"Remember, after the punishment, all is forgiven," Finn said. "Now, how about we get started so we can get to the part where I cuddle you."

Charlotte didn't know what to do. She wanted to get on with this punishment, but she didn't want it. She didn't want to be in pain, and she knew she was going to feel this punishment for days after.

Finn tugged on Charlotte's arm, encouraging her, and that gave her the push she needed to lay herself over his lap. She felt so weird laying there, and so many emotions were running through her.

Charlotte was scared, aroused, and nervous. Scared and nervous because this was her first time getting spanked and aroused because the thought of getting spanked by Finn turned her on.

She had only just met Finn, but she felt the connection with him. She felt a spark had ignited between them.

Finn's hand touched her butt, making her flinch. She didn't expect him to touch her so softly before she got spanked.

"Everything's going to be okay. I'm going to take good care of you," Finn whispered. "Next time you get in trouble, it's a bare bottom for you."

Charlotte gulped and nodded her head. Hopefully she wouldn't get in trouble again, especially when he was around. She didn't want to disappoint him again.

"You have two options. One, you can keep your hands wrapped around my thighs, or I can hold them behind your back. I don't want you moving them to your bottom in the middle of the spanking and getting hurt," Finn said.

"Y-you can hold them," Charlotte whispered.

She didn't trust herself at all to keep her hands from her butt when he started the spanking. She knew once it hurt, she would move her hands.

Finn gently took her hands and placed them together at her lower back, holding them in place with his big hand. Charlotte let out a shaky breath and tensed her body, ready for the spankings to start.

But they didn't come. Hmmm, did he only want to get her in this position and then let her go? Charlotte relaxed over Finn's lap, feeling great that he wasn't actually going to spank her.

Whack.

Charlotte let out a startled yelp and tugged her hands, trying to break them free. The sting of the first spanking brought tears to her eyes. How was she going to make it through the rest of them if it hurt this bad already?

"That was just a warm up," Finn said.

Charlotte struggled in his grip, trying to get off of his lap but failed when he kept her in place.

Several more spankings came, shocking Charlotte before the pain came. She felt like her bottom was on fire.

Finn alternated between cheeks, never hitting in the

same spot twice. Charlotte didn't know how long it went for, and when Finn started to smack her sit spot, she lost it.

Tears streamed down her face as she sobbed. Charlotte tried one last time to get away from his hand, but when it failed, she accepted her fate and laid limp in his lap.

That's when the spankings stopped and she felt herself being picked up. Finn moved her so her bottom wasn't touching anything, but she was tucked against his chest as his arms wrapped around her.

"You did so well," Finn whispered. "It's all over, and all is forgiven."

Charlotte continued to cry in his embrace, letting all of it out. She couldn't stop herself from crying.

"It's okay. Let it all out." Finn rocked them back and forth as he ran his hand up and down her back.

He was soothing her, and it was slowly starting to work as her cries started to calm down. Finn gently ran his hand over her covered bottom, and she let out a cry of pain.

"Nooo," she whined, tears running down her face from the pain. "Stawp! It huwts."

Finn let out a little chuckle and held Charlotte closer to him. "It's supposed to hurt after. It reminds you to be a good little girl *for me and Diana*."

Charlotte looked up at Finn, her tears all dried up now. Her butt was throbbing, and all she wanted to do was put ice on it to make it go away.

"You took the punishment so well. I'm proud of you," Finn said as he stroked her hair.

She relaxed in his embrace and leaned into his touch. It was an awkward position since he was running his hand through her hair, but she didn't care. Finn brought her a sense of peace she didn't realize she needed until now.

Finn gently moved her around his lap so she was laying her head on his chest and her legs were hanging. He held her close to him and slowly rocked back and forth.

"Such a good girl," he whispered as he looked down at her.

A blush covered her face, and she buried her face in his chest, trying to hide from him. She loved it when he called her a good girl. It made her feel all tingly inside, but especially tingly between her legs, and she couldn't help it.

It was his voice, deep and authoritative but calm and soothing all at the same time. It did things to her that had never happened before.

Charlotte's eyes started to droop the longer Finn held her. He was so warm and comfortable.

"Don't fall asleep on me," Finn teased her. "I might have to keep you if you do."

She wanted to tell him that it was tempting. What would it be like to be his? Would she feel cherished and loved? Would he take good care of her but also discipline her when she needed it?

So many thoughts ran through her head when she looked up at him. She wanted to ask him all of those questions and get answers, but she didn't know him that well.

Charlotte didn't want to run him away before she even got to know him. He was her first potential Daddy, and she didn't want to screw it up.

"I want to see you again. Is that alright?" Finn asked, pulling her from her thoughts.

Her eyes went wide before she nodded her head. She couldn't believe that he wanted to see her again.

"Charlotte, I need words." He grabbed her chin to gain her attention.

"Yes, sir," she whispered as she looked into his eyes.

She felt so weird looking into his eyes, but she didn't know where else to look. Charlotte knew if she looked at his lips that thoughts would run through her mind, naughty thoughts.

"Good," he replied with a smile on his face. "Can I see your phone to give you my number?"

She stared at him with wide eyes again, not believing he wanted to give her his phone number. All of this was surreal and it crossed her mind that this might be a dream. A dream she didn't want to wake up from.

Charlotte moved her hand to her arm and pinched herself. She winced from the pain, and Finn's eyes looked alarmed.

"What's wrong? Did I hurt you?" he asked.

"N-no," Charlotte whispered. "I pinched myself."

She was hoping he wouldn't hear that part, but she was wrong when his eyes narrowed on her.

"Why did you pinch yourself?" he asked as he looked at her arm where there was probably a pink, little spot.

"I thought I was dreaming," Charlotte muttered, not looking into his eyes.

"What was that? I didn't hear you."

Charlotte closed her eyes and took a deep breath in. She felt embarrassed. Would that push him away from her?

"Charlotte," Finn warned. "Nothing you say will make me not want to get to know you. You can tell me anything."

She opened her eyes and looked up at him. He was already looking at her with a small smile on his face, encouraging her to tell him.

"I thought I was dreaming," Charlotte said a little louder but not too loud. She didn't want other people to hear her.

"Oh, little one. You aren't dreaming. I'm here with you right now, wanting to get to know you." Finn brushed his hand across her cheek.

Charlotte's head was still resting on his arm and part of his chest. She was relaxed, but she still felt embarrassed that she thought she was dreaming.

"No need to be embarrassed," he said. "I thought I was dreaming when I first saw you. So beautiful and precious. I didn't think you were real until I walked down here and started talking to you."

A blush covered her face at his words. He couldn't mean them, could he?

"Now, I'm pretty sure your friend Diana wants to go home. So I'm going to put my number in your phone, and I'll call you later to set up a time to meet. Unless you want to meet here again if it makes you more comfortable," Finn suggested.

Charlotte nodded her head. "I-I'll have to think about it?" It came out more like a question, but she didn't know what she wanted. She wanted to go out with him to get to know him, but she didn't know if she was comfortable to go somewhere else but the club right now.

She took a shaky breath in. Charlotte didn't have a membership here anymore. Diana had paid for her tonight, and she didn't want that to happen again. That meant they were going to have to meet somewhere else, preferably cheap, so Charlotte could afford it.

"You think about it," Finn said. "Can I see your phone?"

He helped her sit up on his lap. Then Charlotte grabbed her phone out of her pocket and handed it to him. She watched as he put his phone number in and texted himself.

Smart.

Charlotte didn't think she would be able to text him first. She knew nerves would run through her body, and she would psych herself out of texting him.

"Now, be a good girl for Diana. Go home, and get some rest." Finn gave her a hug before setting her on the ground and standing up. "I'll see you soon."

Diana grabbed her hand and started walking toward the front entrance. Charlotte looked back and waved at Finn who was watching them leave. He gave a little wave back right as she walked through the door.

"Did you have a fun time?" Diana asked.

"Yes," she softly spoke.

She really did have a good time, well, until she got spanked.

"Maybe we can come again soon." Diana helped Charlotte into the car.

She stayed quiet, not knowing how to respond. Charlotte wanted to, but she didn't have any money and didn't want Diana to pay for her again. She didn't want to be in debt to her.

The drive to her house was quiet and quick. She didn't live far from the club, which was nice when she was a member.

"Have a good night. I'll pick you up in the morning for work," Diana said.

Charlotte nodded and said goodnight to her before walking up to her door and unlocking it. She walked into her house and to her room.

She didn't want to look at anything in the house right now. Charlotte knew it was a big mess that she needed to clean up, but she couldn't bring herself to do it right now.

Charlotte's phone went off, and she quickly checked it.

It was from Finn.

FINN

Goodnight. Be a good girl, and get some rest!

Charlotte felt butterflies flutter in her stomach, but she also felt anxious. How could she respond to that? Could she respond at all?

She climbed into bed after she placed her phone on the bedside table. Charlotte wasn't going to worry about responding tonight. She needed sleep before she woke up in a couple of hours for work.

She would respond to Finn in the morning when she had time to think over it. With that thought, she found herself closing her eyes and falling asleep.

CHAPTER SIX

FINN

*F*inn watched as Charlotte left the club with her friend Diana. He didn't want her to leave, but he knew she needed to get home. Diana had told her that they needed to leave, and Finn suspected that Charlotte needed to go to bed.

If she was his baby girl, he would be the one taking her home so she could go to bed.

It was getting later by the time they got through the punishment. Finn didn't know where she worked or what time she had to be up, but he just hoped she was able to get enough sleep.

Finn hoped that by giving her a punishment, he didn't keep them here too long. He hoped that she would be able to get enough rest because if she wasn't able to, he knew he would feel guilty for it.

If Charlotte was his baby girl, he would make sure she got at least eight hours of sleep a night so she was well rested. It would be non negotiable because her health was important to him. He wanted a healthy baby girl, but he also knew to have fun at moments. He knew some nights, if she was his, that she wouldn't get eight hours of sleep, but she would definitely have a nap.

Finn was going to text her later tonight to tell her good-night and maybe ask if he could see her again soon. He wanted to get to know her, ask her all sorts of questions, and tell her things about himself. He wanted to take care of her and show her what kind of Daddy he was. He wanted to provide for her and spoil her. He wanted to cherish her. That's all if later on, when they got to know each other, she became his baby girl.

That was all if she was his baby girl, but right now, she wasn't. Maybe soon, but they had just met, and he didn't want to push her into anything if she wasn't ready.

Finn felt deep down that she was the girl for him. He knew when they interacted together that they were meant to be. Now to just see if Charlotte felt the same way as him or not.

Finn thought that she did, but he couldn't be too sure. She could've put up a front and, in reality, had no interest in him. He hoped it wasn't that, but it was a possibility.

But Finn didn't think she was putting on a front around him. She clearly fell into little space, and she was so worried about disappointing him or scaring him off. Not something someone would do if they weren't interested in the person.

His heart broke when she said that because he wanted her to feel as comfortable as possible. He didn't want her to be nervous on how to act around him or that she had to act a certain way.

After he explained that, though, it looked like she let herself go and acted like her normal self. Granted, Finn didn't know if that was actually true, but he wanted to believe that after he said to act normal that she did. Only time would tell when they got to know each other if she actually did or not.

His heart melted when Charlotte turned around while she was walking away to wave at him. She was so cute, and Finn couldn't get enough of her. He loved how she was shy but when she got to talk about something she loved, she would perk up and be animated.

Finn stood up from his chair and walked back to the staircase that led to his office. He needed to sign out of everything before he could go home. He was hoping he wouldn't run into any of the other owners, his friends, before he left.

He didn't want to have to answer any questions, and he also wanted to keep Charlotte to himself right now. Finn knew that Mac had asked about her before he walked down, but he also knew Mac wouldn't say anything to the other seven. It wasn't like him, and he was grateful for that.

Finn walked into his empty office and let out a sigh. He wanted silence to think through everything that had happened in the past two hours. He hadn't thought he was going to find his baby girl any time soon.

Finn thought that he was doomed to be alone forever, being jealous of the people who came in here who had a baby girl, Daddy, or Mommy. He longed for that, and Finn might be getting it soon.

He really hoped he would be getting it soon. This was a time that Finn was glad he worked so many hours before he met her. Now, he had hours that he could put in if he wanted to take time off. Something he wouldn't have been able to do a couple of years ago.

Finn sat down in his chair behind his desk and relaxed for a second. So much had happened in the past two hours, and he wanted to process it all. He needed to process it all.

He loved coloring with Charlotte today; it made him relaxed, but he also felt like he got to know Charlotte as well in that time. Yes, even though they hadn't talked much about anything besides the fact that she loved baked goods.

He would have to watch that later on, if she became his baby girl. He didn't want her to get a tummy ache from eating too much sweets, but he would definitely let her eat some every now and then if she was a good girl.

Finn thought back to when she told her friend Diana no. His soon to be little girl had a little bad side to her. He understood that she wanted to continue to color, but when the person taking care of her said they needed to go, she needed to respect that.

He might have not gone about it that way, but every Dom was different. Finn definitely didn't think he was going to have to discipline Charlotte so early on. A lot of littles acted on their best behavior for the first couple of weeks they got to know a potential Daddy or Mommy, but not Charlotte.

Finn liked that. He didn't want Charlotte to act any differently than how she normally would. He was glad she felt comfortable enough to act herself, even if it was by disobeying her friend who was her 'guardian' in this club.

Finn had looked into that. Charlotte was under Diana's care when they were in the club, and he didn't know how he felt about that. He liked that she was being taken care of, but at the same time, he felt a little off with that, and he couldn't place why.

Finn was kind of glad she acted out because he wanted to

show Charlotte that he wasn't going to let her get away with just anything. Finn had seen too many littles get away with major things, and he didn't like that.

He'd also had littles act one way and then, when he didn't get them in trouble the first time because he gave them a warning, they would go off the wall and be naughty because they thought they could get away with anything.

That wasn't the case, and the little found out pretty quickly that he wasn't like that. Finn always liked to give a warning to them before so they could correct their behavior. He believed in second chances in certain cases, but most of them took advantage of that.

Finn wasn't a super strict Daddy, but he also wasn't that lenient. He was in the middle, and he liked it that way.

If Charlotte acted out, she wouldn't be able to walk all over him. He would hold his ground and punish her if she was his.

Finn couldn't wait for the day she was his, if it ever came. He wanted to be her Daddy for the rest of their lives, but he had to wait a little while. He didn't want to make her uncomfortable; that was the last thing he wanted to do.

He finally had his little girl in his grasp, and he didn't want to do anything to push her away. He wanted to get to know her, take it at her pace, and hopefully it went somewhere.

Finn quickly signed out of everything and shut off his computer. He needed to come in tomorrow to get paperwork done, and he was dreading that. He didn't want to work right now but get to know his soon-to-be baby girl.

He grabbed all of his stuff and walked down the stairs and out of the entrance that led to his parked car. Finn couldn't wait to get home and relax some. He was hoping he could relax, but Finn felt like he was going to be thinking about his baby girl.

That could be relaxing, but Finn also knew that he could start worrying about things in the future. He had done it before, and he would probably do it again soon.

Before Finn turned on his car, he quickly sent a text to Charlotte.

> **FINN**
>
> Goodnight. Be a good girl, and get some rest!

The drive to his house wasn't long at all, and he found himself sitting on the couch as he waited for her response. Finn thought she would have responded by the time he got home, and he started to worry.

Did she get home safely? Did Diana and Charlotte get lost? Did they get into a wreck before they could get home?

So many thoughts went through his brain, and he had to stop himself from going to dark places. Finn took several deep breaths and very slowly calmed himself down.

He didn't need to be thinking like that. First off, she wasn't his baby girl, and she didn't need to respond to him. It would be a courteous thing to reply, but maybe she had a good reason.

She could be asleep since it was late at night. That was a logical explanation that he hadn't thought of at first. His mind always went to the worst at first, and he needed to stop doing that. Not everything turned out extremely bad and he knew that.

Finn got up from the couch and started to get ready for

bed. He knew sitting and waiting for her to reply wasn't going to be good for him. He needed to do something while he waited.

Maybe Finn should've said he would like a text when she got home so he knew she was safe. He had wanted to say that but didn't want to make Charlotte uncomfortable or have Diana intervene.

Finn was going to have to watch out for her friend. He felt like she was going to intervene if she felt like things weren't going to be okay. Finn liked that, but at the same time, Charlotte was an adult and could make decisions for herself.

He wasn't going to do anything bad to her; that was the last thing he wanted to do.

Finn let out a sigh when Charlotte still hadn't responded to him. Maybe she really was asleep. If that was the case, he would text her in the morning to see if they could hang out soon.

With that last thought, Finn got into bed and fell asleep.

CHAPTER SEVEN

CHARLOTTE

*W*ho knew that someone texting a person could throw them off? Charlotte didn't think it was possible for that to happen, but she'd been off all morning. She hadn't replied to Finn last night, and she didn't think he was going to text her until she replied, but she was so wrong, so wrong.

He texted her good morning a couple hours after she woke up. Charlotte didn't reply because she was busy baking, but she was also nervous because she didn't know what to say. Should she ignore the text from last night and just say good morning?

She didn't want to make a fool out of herself, and so she didn't reply again, but now she was making a fool out of herself for not replying. Charlotte had never been good at texting or talking to people.

It had been several hours since he texted her, and she didn't want to reply now because it had been so many hours. It wasn't even morning anymore, that's how long she waited.

Too long.

It had put her in a funk all day, and she didn't know how to get out of it. James even asked if she was okay, and she just silently nodded her head. She didn't know what to say.

It was all getting to be too much for Charlotte, and she didn't know how much more she could take.

It had been weighing on her mind all day, and soon, her shift was going to be over. Then she was going to go home and have all afternoon to think about it for herself.

Charlotte didn't want that, but she didn't have anything else to do. She didn't want to go back to the club in case she saw him after not responding to his text message, twice.

How was she going to make it through this? Did she already lose his interest?

She could feel the anxiety flow through her body with those questions. She felt comfortable around him last night, and he seemed to be genuinely interested in her.

Maybe not anymore since she'd been ignoring him. Charlotte couldn't help it, though, because she'd never had a guy do this, let alone a Daddy, and she didn't know what to do.

Was there a certain way to respond? Did she need to say sir afterwards? Should she call him by his name, or was that disrespectful?

She knew that she couldn't call him Daddy until they'd agreed on him being her Daddy. She knew that much, but besides that, she didn't know what to do. This was the first time someone had actually really taken interest in her, and she was overflowing with anxiety.

Charlotte had talked to other Doms before, but it never went past them talking in the club. Not BTS but a club she went to when she first found out she was a little.

Who knew that talking to someone could bring so much

anxiety? Charlotte didn't know if she liked being so nervous over this.

She was already an anxious person, and this just added more on to it. Not good for her health at all, but she couldn't stop herself. Maybe once they got over this initial talk, she wouldn't be as anxious as she was right now.

"Charlotte," James said, gaining her attention.

Charlotte had also been spacing out a lot today, and she couldn't help it. She was constantly thinking about Finn and how to respond or if she should respond now.

James had caught her several times with a spoon in her hand as she was stirring things, not paying attention to anything. It wasn't a good look for her, and she knew that. She had already made so many messes recently and caused so much trouble.

Charlotte didn't know why James kept her when she struggled so much. He could definitely find somebody that was better suited for this job, but even when she told him all of that, it didn't matter. He told her he wasn't going to fire her, and she kind of was starting to believe that.

If this was any other place, she would have been fired a long time ago. She was lucky, and she knew it. Charlotte didn't know where to go if she ever did get fired. She was already tight on money, and not a lot of places were hiring right now.

She never went to college. She had started to go to culinary school but dropped out when she couldn't afford it. She didn't really have much to her name, and it worried her.

If she ever did get fired, what was she going to do? She couldn't do a lot because she didn't have a bachelor's degree or anything. She only had a high school diploma, and what could you do with that?

"Charlotte," James said again.

"Sorry," she whispered as she looked over at him.

She really needed to get a grip or else he was going to send her home early, again. She couldn't afford to do that. Charlotte knew that they paid her whenever they sent her home early, but she always felt guilty.

She didn't work hard for that money, and she knew that they shouldn't, but they took care of her. It didn't make her feel good that she got paid when she didn't do anything. It made her feel like a charity case, and she wasn't one.

"What has gotten into you? What happened last night, if you don't mind me asking?" James asked.

Charlotte looked down at her feet, not wanting to look into his eyes. She didn't really want to tell James that she potentially had a Daddy interested in her. And she didn't want to say that she might have ruined her chances with him by not responding to his texts.

Tears welled up in her eyes at the thought of all that. The more Charlotte thought about it, the more distressed she got. She didn't want to ruin the chance with Finn, but she felt like she already had.

She had wanted to respond this morning to his text and say good morning, but she was busy, and then she forgot about it for a little bit. They got a rush, and she didn't have time to think about anything else but getting baked goods out.

Maybe if Charlotte had taken a break today like she was supposed to, she could have responded. But she didn't, and now she was regretting it.

"I've got a lot on my mind," Charlotte whispered. She

was hoping that this would keep his questions at bay, but deep down, she knew it wouldn't.

James wanted to help her as much as he could, and that meant he asked a lot of questions.

"Do you need to talk?" James asked.

Charlotte shrugged her shoulders because she wanted to, but she didn't want to make things awkward between her and James. He was her boss after all, and she felt like if she spilled her guts to him about what happened that things would change.

"I don't want to make things weird," she whispered. "I'll talk to my stuffie when I get home."

Charlotte hoped James would understand.

He let out a sigh and knelt down next to her. "If you need anything, let me know. You are an employee, but you're also Amelia's and my friend."

She nodded her head in understanding. They were her friends, but Charlotte always remembered that they were also her employers.

"Well, don't hesitate to call me or Amelia if you need anything," James said as he stood up. "Now, there's a gentleman out in the customer area wanting to talk to you."

Charlotte gave him a confused look. No one ever asked for her or wanted to talk to her while at work. No one knew who she was or that she was even here.

Who could it be?

Curiosity got the best of her, and she peeked her head around the corner, searching the customer area. A pair of eyes were already on her when she looked at the man in a suit.

Taking the person in, Charlotte looked at the man's face. Her eyes went wide, and she ducked, falling to her knees.

Shit.

What was Finn doing here? Charlotte never told him where she worked.

Her knees started to throb from hitting them so hard when she ducked. She shouldn't have done that, but she didn't know what else to do.

Finn was in the bakery and asked to speak to her. Her!

"Charlie?" Finn called out.

Charlotte shook her head even though she knew he couldn't see her. She couldn't see him right now, not after not replying to him all day. What was he going to think?

She thought she had the rest of the afternoon to think about how to respond if she was going to. Now, she didn't even have that.

Finn was here, right now. No more time to think. Maybe Charlotte could slip through the backdoor and get away before he found her back here...but he already knew she was here.

"What are you doing?" Amelia asked.

"Shhh!" Charlotte whispered loudly to Amelia. She didn't want Finn to know she was still here.

Amelia crouched down next to Charlotte. "Why are you on the ground?"

"I'm hiding," she whispered.

Amelia looked around, trying to find who she could possibly be hiding from.

"Do you mean him?" Amelia pointed to Finn, who happened to be a couple of feet away from them.

Charlotte let out a little squeak, and she tried her hardest to get off the floor and into the kitchen. It didn't work smoothly like she wanted to, though.

Her foot slipped on the floor, and it was like everything happened in slow motion. She didn't have enough time to scream or put her hands out in front of her before she crashed against the floor.

"Shit," someone muttered.

Charlotte yelled, fat tears rolling down her face as she laid on the ground. Everything hurt, but her face especially hurt.

Hands wrapped around her body, hauling her off the ground and into someone's arms. Sobs racked her body as the person held her tightly against them.

"You're okay," Finn whispered in her ear. "You're alright."

Charlotte didn't feel alright. Everything hurt, and she couldn't get away from the pain. It was unbearable.

"Huwt," Charlotte mumbled into his chest. "Huwt so bad!"

Finn rocked them back and forth, trying to sooth her as best as he could. After a little while, Charlotte's tears started to slow down and she became more calm.

"Still huwt." She pulled away and pointed to her forehead and cheeks.

"Do you want me to kiss it?" Finn asked.

Charlie nodded her head and leaned forward, waiting for him to kiss her boo-boos okay. He chuckled before leaning forward and kissing her forehead and cheeks.

"All better!" Finn said, giving her a smile.

"Bettew!" Charlie grinned, forgetting all about the pain.

"Charlotte! What happened? Did you slip again?" James barged into the kitchen.

Charlie looked around the kitchen and realized James and Amelia were also here, and her eyes went wide.

Shit. She completely forgot that they were in the bakery. How was she going to explain this to James without making things awkward?

She wiggled in Finn's embrace, wanting to be let down. Just another thing to add on to being embarrassed about later.

How unprofessional of her to be in a man's arms while she was still on the clock.

"I'm so sorry!" she stumbled out. "I didn't mean to!"

CHAPTER EIGHT

CHARLOTTE

*J*ames gave her a disapproving look. "You didn't answer my question. Did you slip again? Are you okay?"

"She did slip and hit her face on the ground," Finn said before she could.

Charlotte glared up at Finn, not liking that he outed her. It wasn't his place to tell James what happened to her. Finn wasn't Charlotte's Daddy yet.

"Don't you dare glare at him," James said.

Charlotte looked over at James and glared at him. She knew she shouldn't be glaring at her boss, but Finn had no right to say that she slipped.

"We both know you wouldn't have told me the truth. Luckily, if this gentleman wasn't here, I would know by the red spot on your forehead," James said.

Charlotte's hand flew up to touch her head, and she winced as pain spread across.

"Owie," she whined.

"I could have told you that was going to happen," Amelia said, giggling behind her Daddy.

Charlotte kept her head down as tears sprung to her eyes. Sometimes Charlotte wasn't the smartest person, but that didn't mean people had to point it out.

"Apologize to her," James said.

Charlotte looked up with wide eyes, not expecting him to tell that to Amelia. Charlotte had never actually seen James scold her, but she knew that Amelia got in trouble.

Amelia was a brat by heart, and Charlotte knew that. They had hung out one time, and Amelia got them in trouble. She wanted to prove to her Daddy that she could go against his rules, talk back to him, and Charlotte got dragged into it.

Charlotte didn't get in too much trouble, but James did give her a big lecture about not doing something like that again. She didn't want to do it in the first place, but Amelia really wanted to and didn't give her much of a choice.

That was the last time they hung out. After that, Charlotte got busy and then came up with excuses about having to clean up the house, go grocery shopping, hang out with Diana, and other things.

Amelia never called her out on it. Maybe she'd caught on and realized that Charlotte didn't want to hang out and was okay with that.

"I'm sowwy," Amelia mumbled, not looking at Charlotte.

"It's okay," Charlotte whispered, but it wasn't.

She already struggled with a lot of things, and when people made fun of her, it made everything so much more difficult. Charlotte felt like she could never fit in anywhere, and she tried so hard.

In the beginning, she would just act like herself, but

people told her that she was annoying, clingy, too emotional, and Charlotte didn't want to be those things. So she started to be less clingy and emotional, and people still didn't like her.

Now, at this point, she just stuck to herself because she didn't want to disappoint anybody else. Charlotte went to the club and played by herself. She went to the bar and drank by herself. If she went out to eat and Diana wasn't there, she would eat by herself.

It was sad, it was lonely, but she'd started to get used to it.

"Now, how'd you slip?" James asked, turning toward Charlotte.

Charlotte looked back down at her feet, not wanting to tell James. How was he going to react when she told him she slipped trying to get away from Finn?

"Wait, before that," James said as he turned toward Finn. "Who are you?"

Charlotte's heart stopped beating as she stared up at Finn. How was he going to introduce himself? Was he going to say that they met at the club last night?

James and Amelia didn't know that Charlotte went to the club, and she wanted to keep it that way. She felt weird if they knew she went there. A ton of people went to that club, but she'd never seen anyone she recognized. And she was thankful for that.

"I'm Finn, a friend of Charlotte's," he said, holding his hand out.

"James, owner of this bakery."

James shook his hand before he turned back to Charlotte with a raised eyebrow. Charlotte took a step back and caved in on herself. She didn't like the look James was giving her.

"Charlotte didn't know I was coming to see her today.

Sometimes she gets a little embarrassed when I show up unannounced. Charlie was trying to hide from me, and when she went to turn around, she slipped and fell," Finn said before Charlotte could say anything.

Her mouth flew open, and she stared at Finn. Did he really just say that?

"Why were you trying to hide from him?" James asked, looking at Charlotte again.

She opened her mouth, ready to give an explanation but quickly shut it when she didn't have one.

"We have some matters that we need to discuss, and Charlotte's been avoiding them," Finn said again.

Charlotte didn't know how she felt about Finn speaking for her. On one hand, she was grateful because she didn't have to think about coming up with a lie or an answer, but on the other hand, she didn't like that he kept talking for her.

It made her feel safe and like he cared for her, but Finn wasn't her Daddy. He shouldn't be doing this.

"Charlotte, can I talk to you alone for a second?" James asked before he looked at Finn. "If you could wait in the customer area, that would be great."

Charlie looked up at Finn and saw that he was hesitant to leave. Did he really care about her that much? Charlotte knew Diana and James cared, but they had known her for years. Finn hadn't even known her for a full day yet.

"It's otay," Charlotte whispered to him.

Finn looked down at her and gave a small smile. His hand came up and held her cheek for a second. "I'll be right out there if you need me."

Charlotte nodded her head and watched as Finn left the kitchen area.

"Charlotte?" James said.

She looked over at him. What did he want to talk about that Finn couldn't be around for? Did something happen, and he was letting her go?

"I'm sorry," she whispered as she looked down at her feet.

"What are you sorry for?" he asked.

"It was inappropriate for me to be in his arms. I've been distracted all day and haven't done a good job."

James kneeled in front of Charlotte and brought her head up with his hand.

"You don't need to apologize. I'm not firing you," James said. "Finn just kept answering for you, and I wanted to make sure he wasn't a friend who was abusive toward you."

Charlotte shook her head rapidly. "He's not like that! Finn is so nice and cares about me!"

James raised his hands in the air. "I didn't mean anything by it. I don't know him, but I wanted to make sure that you're safe."

She let out a sigh and nodded her head. Charlotte completely understood what he was talking about. James didn't know Finn at all, but Charlotte didn't know him really either.

They had just met the previous night, but she felt like she could trust him. It didn't seem like he had a bad bone in his body.

Well, unless dishing out punishments was considered a bad bone in someone's body. Charlotte could get behind that. She knew she needed the punishment for what she did, but he didn't have to give it. He shouldn't have because he wasn't her Daddy.

"Do I need to ask any more questions about him? How long have you known him for?" James asked.

Charlotte went to answer, but she quickly shut her mouth. She didn't want James to kick him out of the bakery, even if Charlotte didn't want to see Finn right now.

Finn had come here to talk to her, so that meant he might still be interested in her. That was what Charlotte thought, but he could also be here to tell her he never wanted to speak to her again.

"Charlotte. How long have you known him for?" James asked again. "Does Diana know him?"

"Yep!" Charlotte happily replied.

James knew Diana and knew that she took care of Charlotte sometimes, so he trusted her. Charlotte didn't know if that was the first time Diana had met Finn, but she could say that Diana knew him.

Charlotte didn't think that Diana would have let Finn spank her if she wasn't comfortable or trusted him. So that meant something.

James relaxed and nodded at his head. "That's good, that's good."

It seemed like he was talking more to himself than to Charlotte, so she didn't reply. Sometimes James did that around her and Amelia. It wasn't all the time, but both of them knew that they didn't have to respond.

"Now, is what you need to talk to him about urgent, or can it wait thirty minutes until your shift is over?" James asked.

"It can wait," Charlotte responded quickly.

If Charlotte could get out of speaking to Finn, she would be fine with that. She didn't know what he was going to say, and she was nervous. Her stomach was all in knots at the thought of him telling her he wasn't interested anymore.

She knew that she ignored him. Well, she got too busy, and then it had been hours since he sent the text, but it was the same thing.

Charlotte was just nervous that her not being able to respond because she was working would upset him or make him not want her anymore. She had men like that before, where they wanted a response immediately, and if they didn't get a response right away, then they felt entitled to punish her.

They were never her Daddies, but they were people she was trying to get to know before they took that leap. They all ended when Charlotte tried to explain that she couldn't always respond right away. That working at the bakery was constant work, and she didn't have time to get on her phone all the time.

They didn't like that answer, and so Charlotte or the guy would end things. It was for the best because they obviously weren't the person for Charlotte, but it did suck. It sucked that they didn't like that she worked and wouldn't respond on time.

"How about you take off of work early. It's only thirty minutes, and I'll pay you for it, so don't worry," James suggested.

Charlotte knew that it wasn't a suggestion that she could deny; James was telling her that she was taking off of work early. Her heart sank at that because she loved working, and yesterday and today he let her off early.

"It's nothing to do with you, but nothing else needs to be baked right now, which means you can go home early. Have that conversation with him," James said, and at the end, he gave Charlotte a look.

The look of 'I know something's going on, and you need to have that conversation' kind of look.

Charlotte let out a sigh and nodded her head. She guessed she was going to take off, but that didn't mean she was going to have the conversation. She was going to try and get out of it.

James got up off the ground and walked out of the kitchen, Amelia falling right behind him. Charlotte took a deep breath in before she gathered her bag and coat.

She walked to the kitchen door and peeked around the corner, trying to find Finn. He was on his phone, not looking anywhere.

Perfect opportunity to leave the bakery.

With that thought in mind, Charlotte tiptoed out of the kitchen and through the customer area. She glanced at Finn several times to make sure that he was still looking on his phone and not her.

Charlotte made it to the front door, and she grinned. She placed her hand on the door knob, but right as she did that, a hand grabbed her shoulder.

"Sneaking away, little one?" Finn asked.

CHAPTER NINE

FINN

Charlotte was too cute trying to sneak out of the bakery. But what she didn't know was that her shoes were squeaking a little and alerted everybody that she was leaving.

It was cute, and Finn played along. He kept his eyes on his phone as she walked to the front door. She was like a little kid trying to sneak a cookie from the cookie jar.

That cute.

Finn had to keep himself from smiling as he watched her. He knew right then and there that if Charlotte became his, she would be a handful. A good handful, but she would keep him on his toes.

His baby girl.

He loved that ring to those words, and he couldn't wait to get to know her. Finn knew that she was special when he first laid eyes on her. And then when he talked to her, it just solidified everything.

"Isn't she cute trying to sneak away?" a girl said.

Finn looked down and saw that it was Amelia, a coworker

of Charlotte's and it looked like the girlfriend of the guy, James, that was in the kitchen with them.

How close was James to Charlotte? Did he have to worry about him, or was it just strictly boss and employee?

"She is," Finn replied as he watched Charlotte get closer to the door.

When he looked back down at Amelia, he found that she was gone, and he shook his head. She reminded him of a little, a naughty little who needed a good spanking.

Finn quietly walked to Charlotte as she touched the door handle. He placed a hand on her shoulder, stopping her from leaving.

"Sneaking away, little one?" Finn asked.

Charlotte's whole body went rigid before she turned around and looked into his eyes. Finn could see the apprehension in her eyes, and he wanted to take that away.

"Can we talk? We have some things to discuss," he said as he took his hand off her shoulder.

Charlotte stood there for a second, blinking several times but not answering him. So many thoughts went through his mind as he waited for her to reply. Was she never interested in getting to know each other? Did Finn get the wrong impression last night when they first met?

Finn didn't want to do anything that she didn't want. Even last night, he knew that she was shy, reserved, maybe even a little bit scared, but that didn't stop him from trying to talk to her.

Did he make a mistake and push too far?

He didn't think so because she willingly gave her phone to him to put his number in. When he mentioned them hanging out sometime soon, she responded.

Finn didn't think that she would have handed her phone or responded in a positive way when he asked those questions and then not want to the next day.

Her friend was there with them last night, which should have made her more comfortable. The two of them seemed comfortable around each other when they walked out, almost like they'd known each other for years and years.

So what could have changed?

"We can talk somewhere in public if it'll make you feel better," Finn said as he tried to ease her worry and hesitation.

He really wanted to talk to her. He wanted to ask why she didn't respond last night or this morning.

Was it because she was busy and already asleep? Was it because she didn't text and preferred to call? Was she weirded out that he texted her good night and good morning?

There were so many things that went through his mind as he tried to come up with a reason for why she wouldn't respond.

Finn also wanted to get to know her. He wanted to know her dislikes and likes. Her favorite color and her least favorite color. Her favorite food and if she had any stuffies. He wanted to know the names of her stuffies and how she liked to spend her time when she was little.

"You can also invite your friend Diana, if you want. I want you to be comfortable if we do talk," Finn said again before she could respond.

It would be weird if her friend was there, but if she needed that, he was willing to do it. He wanted to make her as comfortable as she could be while they talked.

He didn't want to talk to her while she was scared because they wouldn't get to know each other. She would be worried out of her mind the whole time and not really paying attention to anything.

"There's a cafe around the corner," she whispered and looked at her feet.

Finn almost missed it, but he managed to catch it.

"Great! Do you want to call your friend?" Finn asked.

He waited for Charlotte to answer before they went anywhere. If she wanted her friend, they would wait in the bakery while she drove over here.

"No, it's okay," Charlotte said as she looked up at Finn.

Finn opened the door and ushered Charlotte out. He knew where the cafe was that was around the corner. He'd lived in this city for over ten years now and had gone to several different cafes.

He loved his coffee, and so when he first moved here, he wanted to find a place where he could get it. The cafe around the corner was one of the three places he liked to get his coffee.

Charlotte walked out of the bakery and onto the sidewalk, closer to the road. Finn immediately felt a little panic flow through his body.

He quickly placed his hand on her shoulder and guided her toward the inside of the sidewalk. His parents taught him right when he was growing up that a woman should never be on the outside of the sidewalk.

"Why'd you do that?" Charlotte asked as she looked up at him.

"Whenever we're together, I'm always on the outside," Finn said, leaving no room for discussion.

"Why?"

"Because if the car were to get out of control, I would be

able to see and protect you. I would take the brunt of the hit before you did."

Charlotte stayed silent as they walked. Was he too forward with that? Should he have been kinder when he explained it?

The cafe came into view, and they walked a little faster, well, Charlotte walked a little faster. Finn opened the door for Charlotte and they made their way in.

"What would you like?" Finn asked.

Charlotte rocked on her feet as she looked on the menu. "Hot chocolate? No, I'll have tea. Wait."

Finn let out a chuckle. "If it helps, you can have one now, and before we leave, I'll get you the other one."

Charlotte's face lit up as she looked at him. Her eyes sparkled with excitement, and she giggled.

"Tea now, then hot chocolate," she said.

If Finn hadn't met her last night, he would have thought that she was little at this point. The way she acted around him and the way she spoke back in the bakery all presented that she was a little.

Thankfully, he didn't have to think if she was or not because she was at the club last night.

"Great! Why don't you go find a seat, and I'll order the drinks," Finn suggested.

He watched as Charlotte skipped over to an empty table and sat down. He could watch her all day because she was that cute.

Finn quickly ordered a hot tea and a black coffee for himself before he walked over and sat down in front of Charlotte. Right as he sat down, she went rigid and started to play with her fingers.

67

He made her nervous, and Finn didn't know if he liked that or not. Was she nervous because she liked him? Or was she nervous because of what he was going to talk to her about?

Finn wanted it to be because she liked him, not because they had things to discuss. He didn't like making people nervous and anxious. He knew sometimes it was unavoidable, but he tried to make people as comfortable as possible.

"Take a couple deep breaths in," Finn said. "It always helps me calm down when I'm anxious."

Charlotte gave him a tight, thin smile but took several deep breaths in.

"I want you to know that what we're going to talk about is nothing bad. I just want to know why because I thought we had a connection last night," Finn said right before the waiter came and dropped their drinks off.

Before Charlotte could grab her drink, Finn took it, opened the lid, took a straw and dumped it in before placing a little tea on the back of his hand. Cafes were notorious for having drinks way too hot, and he didn't want Charlotte to get burnt.

Charlotte watched in fascination as he did this.

"Perfect temperature," Finn said as he placed the lid back on her drink.

"Thank you," she quietly said.

"Why didn't you respond to my texts?" Finn asked. "Did I make you uncomfortable?"

Charlotte stared at him with wide eyes. She opened her mouth several times and closed it. If this was any other situation, Finn would have found it amusing. She was at a loss of words, but right now, he didn't find it amusing.

In the beginning, Finn thought that she might have not gotten home all right last night. But that quickly passed when he remembered her friend took her home. It eased some of his worry but not all of it.

His only other thought was that he made her uncomfortable somehow. That wasn't his goal, and if he did, he wanted to clear it up.

"Were you asleep when I texted you last night?" Finn asked.

Charlotte looked down at her drink. "I was about to go to bed, and I tried not to get on my phone."

Finn could tell that she was telling the truth, and he was glad she didn't get on her phone right before she went to bed.

"I was gonna respond this morning, but I was running late for work, so I didn't," Charlotte said quickly. "And then. And then. And then."

Finn watched as Charlotte stumbled over her words. He seemed to think that any time she got super nervous or tried to talk really fast she stuttered over her words.

He thought it was cute that whenever she got flustered, excited, nervous that she stuttered over her words, but at the same time, he felt sad because right now he knew that she was nervous.

Finn didn't want Charlotte nervous.

"It's okay, take a deep breath in. Let it out. That's it. Take another deep breath in, and let it out slowly," Finn instructed her, and she followed what he said.

Charlotte calmed down, and a blush took over her face. He loved that he made her blush. He could get used to seeing her cheeks rosy red.

"And then I got busy working when you texted the

second time and didn't have time to reply. And by that point, I hadn't replied to either one of them for several hours, and I thought it was just better not to respond," Charlotte said, looking down at her hands.

Finn took a deep breath and nodded his head.

"I want you to know that even if you don't respond for hours because you're working doesn't mean I don't want you to reply. If you were my little girl, I would expect a reply," Finn said.

Charlotte's head moved back, almost like a flinch, and it caught Finn's attention. What did he say to make her react that way? Was it when he said if she were his little girl? Was that a step too far?

"I don't expect an answer right away because I know work comes first, but I would like a response. Even a short text saying you're at work is fine. I just want to know that you're okay and safe," Finn said.

Charlotte finally looked into his eyes, and he saw so many emotions swirling in her eyes. He wanted to know what she was thinking.

Was he going all wrong about this? Should he have talked to her last night about responding?

"What are you thinking? Give me all your unfiltered thoughts," Finn said, catching her off guard.

CHAPTER TEN

CHARLOTTE

So many emotions went through Charlotte as Finn spoke. He wanted her to respond to him, even if it was hours after he sent the text because she was working. Not a lot of people had told her that.

Charlotte especially couldn't do that when she was the main baker, the only baker. It had been tough on Charlotte when she got to know a lot of different guys only to have to tell them it wasn't going to work out because they expected a response immediately.

Granted a lot of the guys that she was getting to know all wanted her to be a stay-at-home wife. Charlotte wouldn't mind being a stay at home wife, if it was her choice, but the guys wanted to force it on her, and right now, Charlotte wanted to work at the bakery.

She loved working there so much. It gave her purpose in life right now. Though, she had to work right now because she desperately needed money. She was already struggling for money, and she was working forty hours a week.

Something needed to change, but Charlotte didn't know

what. She had never been good at money or tracking where she bought things. Charlotte had been trying really hard the past month to track and make sure she was only buying things she absolutely needed.

But somehow she still didn't have enough money. Charlotte got rid of her membership at the club, she only bought a couple of staple food items each week, she didn't buy anything for her little side—except for the shopping—, and she tried to walk to work when she could. Well, when Diana couldn't take her.

But even when she did all that, she still didn't have enough money. It seemed like her electric bill was going up and her water bill was skyrocketing, but she took quick showers so that she didn't use a lot, and she didn't leave a light on for too long.

Well, she had a night-light that she used every night because she was afraid of the dark, but the guy at the store said it wouldn't take up a lot of electricity.

Charlotte had thought about asking Diana to look over her bank account with all her receipts that she had kept and see where it was going. But Charlotte didn't want Diana to worry about her, and she didn't want Diana to take pity on her and give her money.

That was the last thing Charlotte wanted.

Now she was here sitting in front of Finn. He was talking to her, trying to make sense of why she didn't respond. Then he said that he expected a reply, and that didn't sit well with her.

Was it going to be like every other guy she had talked to? Wanting a response right away.

It was like he knew what she was thinking because then

he talked about how it didn't need to be right away because he knew she worked. Charlotte didn't know what to believe.

Finn sounded genuine when he said those words, but she knew better. So many times guys had said the exact same thing, but they did want a response right away.

Maybe Charlotte was better off without a Daddy or significant other. Recently, Charlotte had even thought about having a vanilla guy to try and find a potential significant other, but it still wasn't working.

They all wanted her to respond right away. In the beginning, she tried to respond right away, but when Charlotte fell into little space, she wasn't on her phone. That was the last thing on her mind, and none of the vanilla guys could understand that. They didn't know that she was a little.

Maybe Finn was different. Maybe he truly didn't mind that she worked and wouldn't be able to respond right away. Charlotte didn't know, and she didn't know how to ask or make sure that he really meant what he said.

She didn't want to sound rude or doubtful, but she was doubtful. She had so many men tell her one thing but then get mad when they said that it was okay. Charlotte wasn't about that, and she didn't want it to happen again.

"What are you thinking? Give me all your unfiltered thoughts," Finn said.

Charlotte stared at Finn in shock. She had so many things to say, and she didn't know where to start. She wanted to tell him her doubts and her concerns, but she didn't want to scare him off.

One time a guy had told her to tell him what she was thinking, and when she did, he didn't like it. Charlotte was being honest, and he didn't want that. He wanted to hear what he wanted to hear, and she said the opposite.

"I promise I really want your unfiltered thoughts so that I can follow along on what you're thinking. It won't hurt my feelings if you say something," Finn said, bringing Charlotte out of her thoughts.

It was like he knew exactly what to say to her at the right time. Almost like he could read her thoughts.

Charlotte's eyes went wide at that thought, and she looked up at Finn.

"Can you read my thoughts?" she whispered, waiting for his answer.

What if he could?

Finn chuckled and shook his head. "I can't read your thoughts."

Her shoulders sagged in relief, and she let out the breath she was holding. That was a relief, Charlotte thought to herself. She didn't know what she was going to do if he could read her thoughts.

He would know her past relationships and how she was so nervous to be around him.

"I can read your body language and your facial expressions," Finn said. "You're like an open book sometimes. It helps me because then I know what you could possibly be thinking."

"Like what?" Charlotte found herself asking.

"Just because you're asking these questions doesn't mean you're not going to answer mine, but I'll answer first, and then you can answer mine," Finn said, giving Charlotte a wink and a smile.

Charlotte thought her stomach sank when he realized

what she was doing. She was hoping that he wouldn't notice, but nothing seemed to get past him. He always seemed to know when she was trying to deflect.

"You have these little ticks, we'll call them. When you're nervous, you won't make eye contact with me, and you'll start playing with your fingers. Your body goes rigid, and you look uncomfortable. You flinch sometimes when people say something or you're thinking something in your head, and you don't realize it. You wear your emotions on your face sometimes," Finn said.

Charlotte's mouth hung open the longer he talked. She didn't think that he was observing her that much, but she was obviously wrong. He had obviously spent his time watching her and seeing how she reacted and acted.

"Now, I want to hear your unfiltered thoughts about what I said." Finn relaxed in his chair.

Charlotte opened her mouth, ready to spill everything she had thought about, but she quickly closed her mouth. Was she really about to do this? Was she really ready to tell him what she thought?

"It's okay. Take your time," Finn said.

He grabbed her hand that was laying on top of the table and gently rubbed his thumb across the back of her hand. It was soothing, and it calmed her down some. She didn't realize that she had started to get wound up and tight, but he could tell.

He could tell things when she couldn't; he was observant, and she kind of liked that. Sometimes Charlotte could get into her own head and go down a dark path. Not many people realized when she started to do that, but Finn saw it.

Charlotte let out a sigh and looked down at her hands.

"I've had a lot of people tell me the exact same thing you are telling me. They never worked out because they were just saying it to say it, but they didn't mean it."

Charlotte didn't want to tell Finn any of this, but she knew that he wouldn't let this go, and she needed to say something. How was anything going to work if she never talked about her past experiences and moved on from them?

She obviously had been scarred by what the men said and did. She kept telling herself that she wasn't affected by their words, but she was. How could she not be when so many of them said the exact same thing but didn't mean it.

Finn gave a sad smile and Charlotte's hand squeeze. "Well, I do mean it. I know that people work to make a living, and that means that they may not be able to respond always. I can't always respond right away."

That was another thing that the men would always say. That they understood but then they would get angry when she didn't respond right away. They would say that they understood because they worked too and couldn't always respond right away.

Sometimes those men would not respond for a day or two because they were 'busy', but Charlotte never felt like it was because they were busy. She sometimes felt that they would not respond for several days because they realized she couldn't text back right away, so they weren't interested anymore. Or they realized that she wanted to continue to work, and they didn't want that.

"A little communication goes a long way for me. Just a simple I'm busy for the next couple of hours or a text before you go into work saying that you're working until whatever time would be great. I just want to know that you're safe and that you're okay," Finn said. "We're still in the talking phase, but I want to get to know you better and your little side."

Charlotte blushed and looked even further down to try and hide it. She had only blushed a handful of times, and most of them had been with him. He just did something to her. Charlotte didn't know if it was the dominance, the Daddy side, his handsomeness, his genuineness, or just him.

She never had somebody affect her so much, and she didn't know what to do. It was all new to her, and she didn't know how to navigate through it.

"I want you to be comfortable. I want you to not worry that you haven't responded to me in several hours because of work and that I will not be interested in you any more. I can guarantee you that I'm very interested, and you not responding for a couple of hours because you're busy at work won't make me feel any different," Finn said.

Charlotte's heart melted as Finn continued to speak. He knew exactly what to say, and everything seemed to be genuine. Maybe Charlotte should give him a chance to prove that he wasn't just saying this to say it like all the other guys did, but that he meant it.

She opened her mouth, ready to tell him that she also wanted to get to know him, but stopped herself. Charlotte needed to think about this because every time a guy had wanted to get to know her, she just jumped right in.

Charlotte needed to take a day or two to see if she was really interested in Finn like that. She already knew the answer, but she needed to do this. Diana would tell her the exact same thing. She was always saying that she needed to think more before doing something, and right now, she was going to do that.

Now Charlotte just needed to tell Finn. How was she going to tell him? She didn't want to hurt his feelings and make it seem like she wasn't interested because she was, but she also didn't want to jump right in.

She didn't want to get her hopes up again.

"How about you think about everything for the next couple days? Then once you have your answer, we can meet up again and talk about it, and if it's positive, then we can get to know each other at the same time," Finn suggested.

Before Charlotte knew what she was doing, she nodded her head.

"Otay," Charlotte whispered.

The dominant voice Finn used made her fall into little space easier. Charlotte had fallen into little space more in the past couple of days than she had in a while.

So much for trying to keep her little locked away.

Finn gave her a smile. She could get used to that smile. It made her insides all gooey.

Charlotte watched as Finn looked down at his watch, and his eyes went a little wide.

"I need to go to work because I have some admin stuff to do. Can I drop you off at your house?" Finn asked.

Charlotte felt sad that he already had to go. She wanted to hang out with him some more, but he needed to leave. She also didn't know how to feel about him wanting to drop her off.

Diana wasn't supposed to pick her up today, which meant she had to walk home, but Charlotte didn't really want to walk home right now. She also didn't want to call Diana and ask her to come pick her up.

Diana would ask so many questions, and she wasn't up for answering them right now. Charlotte just wanted to go home, think about things, and procrastinate on doing adult things.

"Charlotte?" Finn said.

She looked up at him and nodded her head. She didn't have enough money to get a taxi to drive her home, and she didn't want to walk, so having Finn drive her was her best option right now.

He gave her a big smile and stood up. Finn grabbed their cups and threw them away before he grabbed Charlotte's hand and walked them out.

"Do you still want your hot chocolate?" Finn asked.

Charlotte had completely forgotten about how she wanted hot chocolate afterwards, but right now, she didn't want it.

"No, thank you," she whispered.

Finn helped her into his car, reaching across her to buckle her in before shutting her door and walking around to his side.

Charlotte loved that even though he wasn't her Daddy right now, he still took care of her. It made her realize how much she wanted to have her own Daddy. What she was missing out on.

"Address?" Finn turned toward Charlotte as he turned on the car.

Charlotte rattled off her address, and they started heading to her house in complete silence. It wasn't a bad silence; it was really comfortable, and Charlotte was thankful for that.

Before she knew it, Finn had parked right in front of her

house. Charlotte unbuckled herself and got out of the car, a little disappointed that Finn didn't help her out.

"Charlotte," Finn gained her attention.

She turned around and saw that Finn was out of the car and near her.

"Next time you're with me, you don't get out of the car alone. I'll always help you in and out," he said.

She looked down at her feet in embarrassment. She should have known better, but she wasn't thinking.

Finn grabbed her hand and walked her up to her door. He waited until she had unlocked the door before speaking.

"Maybe in the next couple of days, we can meet up and you can give me your answer?" Finn asked.

Charlotte knew that she was going to have her answer before then, but she nodded

"I would like that," she replied.

"Have a good rest of your afternoon, and don't go to bed too late," Finn said as he took a step back.

Charlotte walked into her house, giving Finn a little wave before closing the door. All she wanted to do was open it again and tell him that she wanted to get to know him, but she needed to think.

She leaned up against the closed door and took several deep breaths. Charlotte had a feeling deep down that Finn was going to be her Daddy.

CHAPTER ELEVEN

FINN

He had been sitting at his desk for the past hour. It had been a slow and painful hour in the office away from Charlotte. Finn wanted to stay with her for a couple more hours, but he knew he needed to get this paperwork done.

This paperwork was time sensitive, and if he didn't get it done soon, then BTS could lose a lot of money. Finn didn't want that, and he knew his friends and other owners wouldn't like it either.

He had told the other owners that he would get it done, but he had procrastinated on it. Finn didn't know that he was going to find his future baby girl the other day. If he would've known, he wouldn't have procrastinated on doing this paperwork.

This was the next step for the business. This was their baby, and they wanted to see it thrive.

"How's the paperwork for expansion going?" Mac asked as he walked into Finn's office.

All nine of them had a brief talk about expanding the

club. They wanted to build another one in a different city where their friend was. Apparently there were a lot of Daddies, Mommies, and littles who wanted a club just dedicated for them.

Finn never imagined that their club would have gotten as big as it was now. It started out as a passion project, and none of them really thought there would be a huge market in Springfield, Missouri, but they were proven wrong.

The club had a lot of people who came from all over the world to visit. The nine owners got at least ten emails a week saying that people wanted a club in their own city. After a few years, Finn and his friends were finally trying to expand.

"I shouldn't have procrastinated on it. I should've gotten it done right when we got all the paperwork," Finn said as he ran his hands over his face.

He wanted to be anywhere but the club right now. He wanted to be with Charlotte, getting to know her, but he knew, even if he didn't have this paperwork to fill out, he still wouldn't be able to hang out with her.

He needed to give her time to think about everything. Finn didn't want to be overbearing and coerce her into being with him; that was the last thing Finn wanted.

"I told you not to, but you didn't pay attention." Mac sat down on the couch in front of Finn's desk. "Granted, if you asked any of us, we would've taken over since you've found your potential little."

Finn looked up at Mac and gave him a mocking smile, not amused. Mac liked to rub anything and everything in when he was right. He was the one that was almost always right, and he made sure people knew it.

"Have you seen the cutie today?" Mac asked.

"She's got a name," Finn grumbled.

"So tell me her name."

Sometimes Finn didn't like Mac, and right now was one of the times. Mac could be pushy, and this was one of the instances when he felt like being pushy. Finn knew to tell him the truth unless he wanted to sit here for the next couple of hours as Mac asked over and over again until he got the answer.

"Finn, tell me. I'm not going to steal her from you. I've got my eyes on a little already." Mac relaxed into the couch.

Finn's eyebrows rose at that news. Mac wasn't the type of person to stay with anyone. He was a player and loved that life.

"You've got your eyes on a little? When did that happen?" Finn asked. He hoped to deflect the questions onto Mac.

Mac grinned and shook his head. "I'll tell you if you answer my questions about little miss cutie from the other night."

Finn let out a sigh. He knew Mac would answer his questions after Finn answered his.

"Fine, I'll answer your questions, and then you answer mine," Finn agreed.

He really didn't want to answer Mac's questions, but he was curious about the little who caught his attention. It was so unlike Mac, and he wanted to be the first to hear about it.

"Did you get to see the cutie today? What's her name?" Mac asked with a smug look on his face.

"Her name is Charlotte, and I did get to see her today," Finn replied, giving the bare minimum. "We hung out for an hour before I had to come here and get this paperwork done before it's too late."

Mac whistled and shook his head. "You should've called one of us. We would've done it for you while you hung out with her."

Finn let out a sigh. "If I could, I would've, but I need to give her time to think about things."

"Talk."

Finn knew he shouldn't have said that, but he couldn't stop himself. He didn't want to go into the details of how he had texted her and she didn't respond. How she felt bad for not responding because she was working and so she just decided not to respond. He didn't want to say that she might not want him to be her Daddy.

"You can't get out of this. I'll talk about mine if you talk about yours, and I don't want just some half-ass answers. I want you to explain because there's obviously something going on, and you don't seem as excited as you should be," Mac said as he sat up straighter on the couch.

Mac was also a good listener, and Finn knew that whatever he told him he would keep to himself. He didn't have to worry about him going to any of the other seven and blabbing his mouth, and he appreciated that.

Finn let out a sigh. He knew that he needed to talk to somebody about this to see if they could see it from a different light. He felt an instant connection with Charlotte and knew after less than a day that she was his baby girl, but she had been hesitant.

Granted, it had only been a day, but Finn knew, and when someone knew, someone knew.

"We exchanged phone numbers last night, and I texted

her good night, but I didn't get a response. I thought she might have already been asleep. Then I texted her this morning, telling her good morning, and she never responded," Finn started to explain. "I got a little worried, and so I looked up her profile, but she didn't give a phone number for herself, only her friend Diana's phone number."

Finn felt like a teenage boy at this point, talking about his school girl crush, but he knew that this wasn't just a crush. This was his future baby girl, and he didn't want to mess this up.

"Go on," Mac said.

"So I called Diana, and she told me that Charlotte was at work and gave me the address, so I went over there to see if I could talk to her and find out if she wasn't interested anymore or what was going on." At this point, Finn got up from his chair and started to walk around the room. "I talked to her boss, and he said she would be out soon. I caught sight of her, and when I did, she ducked, so I went to investigate. When she saw that I knew where she was, she tried to get up and bolt, but she slipped and hit her head."

That had Mac sitting up even straighter than he was before. "Is she okay?"

If you told any Daddy Dom that a little fell, they would all be worried. It was nice that they all cared and that even if they already had a little or didn't, they would still care.

Finn let out a sigh and nodded his head. "She cried a lot, but I got her to calm down. We then went out and had a conversation, and long story short, she was super worried that since she didn't respond because she was at work that I wanted nothing to do with her."

"Did she say that out loud?"

"Yes, she did, and I could also see it all in her body language. I repeatedly told her that it was okay that she didn't respond because of work and that I didn't expect her to respond right away, but I did expect a response."

"So what's the problem?"

"She seems hesitant about everything. I don't know if she's ever had a Daddy of her own. She had such an uncertain look on her face that before she could speak, I told her she could have a couple of days to think about everything before we proceeded."

Finn felt like that was a mistake, but he knew it wasn't. He wanted to tell her that he could see she wanted him, that she needed a Daddy, but he didn't want to overstep his boundaries. He didn't want to coerce her into anything or demand that she be with him.

"So are you worried that she's going to say no?" Mac asked.

Finn shook his head. "I don't think she's going to say no. I think she's going to say yes but just needs some time to think about it. I hope she does because I know she's the one."

Mac chuckled and shook his head.

"What?" Finn asked.

"I've just never seen you like this. Sure you've had littles before, but you've never been this serious. You've only known her for twenty-four hours, and you already know that she's the one?" Max said. "It's just different. What's next, you're going to cut your hours and not work as much if she says yes?"

Finn had already thought about that. If Charlotte said yes to him, he was going to cut some of his hours and take vacation time to hang out with her and get to know her.

"If she says yes, I'll probably take half days so that I can hang out with her in the afternoon and get to know her," Finn said as he stopped walking and looked at Mac.

Mac's face turned to shock, and he stood up from the couch. "I'm happy for you. I really am because you deserve this. You've gone a long time without a little, without taking care of someone, and put all this work into the club. It's time that you got a break, that you had someone."

Finn agreed with him. He was glad that he worked so hard the past couple of years and saved up all this money. Now he could take vacation time and spoil his little girl if she said yes.

He couldn't wait for the day when he got to spoil his little girl. It could be tomorrow, the next week, or a couple of months from now, but he couldn't wait.

"Well, I've gotta go get some work done," Mac said as he walked toward the door.

"Ah, ah, ah. Don't you dare walk out of this office. You said fair trade, and you don't go back on your word," Finn said.

Mac wasn't going to get off this easy. Finn wanted to know who this little girl was that caught Mac's attention, and he was going to find out.

Mac turned around and gave Finn a smile. "I was hoping you would forget about that, but I can see that you obviously didn't."

"You're not getting off that easily. I want to know who caught your attention because nobody has done that before." Finn sat on the edge of his desk.

"Fine, I'll tell you. There isn't much to say because I haven't talked to her much," Mac said as he leaned up against the wall. "She's been coming to the club for a couple of years. She's had Daddies off and on but nothing ever serious. She's always caught my attention, but I didn't know how to approach her because she always had a Daddy."

"So it changed now?" Finn asked.

"I knew she didn't have a Daddy, so I walked up to her and asked if I could play with her, and she said yes. So I played dolls with her for a couple of hours before she had to go home. The best time of my life, well, best time this last week. I've gotten to know her a little, but we haven't talked much, and she hasn't been back in a while."

"Could she be out of town?"

"I don't know what she does for work, and I didn't want to look up her phone number and ask because I want to gain her trust and not break it by looking up her information. I'm hoping she comes to this huge little event we're holding so that I can talk to her and see if we can get to know each other better."

"That's a good idea! I need to ask Charlotte if she wants to go to that."

Mac chuckled. "Maybe wait until after she says yes or no."

Finn knew that already. He was already going to wait until after Charlotte said yes, if she said yes.

"Well, I hope your little one comes," Finn said.

All but two of the owners didn't have littles.

"Well, I really got to go now. I've got to talk to somebody about cupcakes we are ordering for the littles' event. Well, not talk to somebody but I need to make sure that we're getting enough and that the time is correct and all that fun stuff," Mac said as he opened the door.

"Have fun with that," Finn replied.

Mac walked out of his office and left Finn to his thoughts. All Finn needed to do was finish this paperwork, and then he didn't have to think about anything else.

He groaned as he sat down in his chair again. He really didn't want to do this paperwork, but he knew he needed to. With that last thought, Finn started working to try and get it done.

CHAPTER TWELVE

CHARLOTTE

It had been a couple of days since Finn and Charlotte talked at the coffee shop. Charlotte had been busy with work and had been so tired; she knew that if she hung out with anyone, she wouldn't have been able to pay attention.

Finn wanted to meet up and talk about things, but Charlotte told him that she was exhausted and just wanted to sleep. He understood and told her to get some much needed rest and to not stay up too late.

All Charlotte wanted to do was hang out with him, but she knew she would be no good in her state. She wanted someone to take care of her when she got back from work but didn't know who to ask.

Finn wasn't her Dom or Daddy Dom, and she didn't want to call Diana and bother her. Charlotte didn't like bothering people with tasks that she could do. She didn't need a Daddy Dom, but she wanted one.

She wanted to feel cherished and loved, taken care of by

a Daddy, but she didn't need it. What Charlotte needed was money because she was always struggling.

Charlotte had called Finn last night and told him that she wanted to get to know him. She had thought about it for a couple of days and knew that she wanted to take a step forward.

Charlotte knew from the beginning when they talked in the coffee shop that she wanted to get to know him, but she didn't want to rush into anything. She had a habit of doing that, and it was not turning out well.

It took everything in her not to call Finn the next morning and tell him that she wanted to get to know him more, to tell him that she wanted him to be her Daddy.

It was still taking a lot in her not to call him and tell him exactly that. She had gotten told several times to have ten seconds of courage and just do or say what she meant to do or say. Charlotte had thought about having those ten seconds of courage to tell Finn that.

She'd never had a Daddy, so she didn't know what she was really missing out on. Yes, she had seen Amelia interact with her Daddy, but besides that, she hadn't seen much. However, she'd read countless books that made her crave having a Daddy even more.

Finn and Charlotte were meeting up today to talk about some things. Charlotte was nervous about the meetup, and she didn't know how much she was going to be able to pay attention. She was still catching up on her sleep.

No matter how hard Charlotte tried to fall asleep at night, she couldn't. She hugged her stuffies, got into her pajamas, but sleep never came. She had kept waking up in the middle of the night and was not able to fall back to sleep.

It was not really good for this to be happening to Charlotte because she woke up so early—her day started early so that she could bake goodies for people that came in during the morning rush.

Charlotte enjoyed baking little treats for people because normally it brightened up their day, but it sucked that she hadn't been able to sleep well recently. She thought in the beginning it could be because of Finn and how she was nervous around him. How she wanted to give him an answer but didn't want to rush into anything.

Charlotte thought it would get better once she told Finn she was interested in getting to know him better, but it hadn't. If anything, it had gotten worse. She didn't know how to combat this because she'd never had to deal with it before.

She didn't want to disappoint Finn with her thoughts or how she acted. She wanted to be perfect for him, and she didn't know how to be. Deep down, Charlotte knew that he wouldn't be disappointed, but she didn't know that for sure.

From what she'd seen and read, every Daddy was different with their littles. Part of her nervousness was that Charlotte didn't know how Finn was when he was a Daddy.

Was he strict or more lenient? Was he affectionate or hard? Did he love giving out discipline at every chance or did he not?

Charlotte didn't know the answer to any of those questions, and it was making her stressed. She liked to know things, and her anxiety had worsened by not knowing.

She knew that she could just ask him, but she hadn't had the time. She was also nervous that if she asked, he wouldn't like it.

So many things to think about and Charlotte was getting overwhelmed with everything.

Finn had texted her earlier this morning that he wanted to talk about something tonight. That made Charlotte worry even more. What if he wasn't interested any more? What if he wanted to stop seeing her because she had those doubts and he knew them?

Charlotte set down her frosting tip and let out a sigh. She had just finished decorating two hundred cupcakes for an event. She didn't know what the event was, only that they ordered so many cupcakes and the people wanted them colorful.

James had told her, and Charlotte couldn't keep her excitement in. She loved it when people didn't give her many parameters when it came to decorating things. Charlotte loved letting her creativity go wild, and she knew she could do it this time because they said they wanted them colorful.

"How are they coming along?" James asked as he stood in the doorway.

Charlotte wiped her forehead with the back of her hand. "I just finished decorating them. Just in time for you to take them."

James cleared his throat. "I wanted to talk to you about that."

She knew something was going to come up when he said that. James never said that without something going on, something she wasn't going to like.

"Yes?" Charlotte said.

"I need you to deliver them for me," James replied.

Charlotte's heart sank when he said those words. James knew that she wouldn't like this, and yet he suggested it. He knew that Charlotte didn't like to deliver things to customers. She was nervous that she would make a mistake or say something wrong and the customer would never want to work with them again.

Sometimes Charlotte couldn't hold back her words, and so she tried her best not to interact with customers too much. She didn't want to ruin the reputation that James had worked so hard to create. Everyone loved this bakery, and she didn't want to be the reason that people started to hate it.

"I wouldn't ask you this if I didn't have a good reason. I have a guy coming in for an interview, and today was the only day he could come in, so I can't deliver them. You know that Amelia doesn't have a driver's license, so she can't. I don't have anyone else to deliver them besides you," James explained. It didn't help, though. Charlotte still didn't like it. "I'll give you a little bonus for delivering them!"

Charlotte thought about it for a second. She needed all the money she could get, and she knew his bonuses were generous when it came to things she didn't like to do. This wasn't the first time he'd asked her to do something she wasn't comfortable with or didn't like to do.

She let out a sigh and nodded her head. "Okay."

Charlotte had a bad feeling about this. Delivering two hundred cupcakes shouldn't be that hard. That was what Charlotte thought, but she didn't really know. She had never delivered that many before.

"Thank you. I owe you on top of giving you a bonus!" James said. "Here's the address, and Amelia will help you put all the cupcake boxes in the van."

James handed her the piece of paper, and Amelia showed up behind him. It didn't take long for Amelia and Charlotte to load up all the cupcakes in the van, but by the time they were done, they were out of breath.

"I never want to do that again," Amelia whined.

"Me too!" Charlotte agreed. "Hopefully the interview goes well for the guy, and he gets hired. Maybe he'll do all the lifting and placing things in the van. Give us a break."

Amelia agreed before she wished Charlotte good luck and walked back into the bakery. Charlotte was on her own now, and she didn't like it.

She never liked it when she was on her own, and yet she found herself being on her own more and more.

Charlotte got into the van and put the address into her phone. Her eyebrows rose when BTS came up. Why are they wanting two hundred cupcakes? In the years she was a member, they never bought cupcakes.

Maybe this was for the staff and owners of the club. They could be having a get together, but did they have two hundred people that worked there? Maybe Charlotte could ask Finn if she saw him there.

She was a curious person, and she wouldn't be able to stop thinking about it until she figured out what these cupcakes were for.

Charlotte drove to the club and sat in the parking lot for several minutes. Anxiety rolled through her body, and it rooted Charlotte to her seat. She didn't want to get out and deliver the cupcakes. She hated talking to people, and she was going to have to talk to someone.

Maybe luck would be on her side and she would see Finn. Was Finn even working right now? Charlotte didn't know what hours he worked. Should she text him to see if he was there?

Charlotte shook her head. No, she couldn't. What if he wasn't and he came in for her? She didn't want him to do that. They were going to see each other later today.

Charlotte told herself she needed to be a big girl right now. She had to be because no one else was going to be. She took a deep breath in and let it out slowly before she opened her door and got out of the car.

She could do this. It wasn't the first time she had to do something like this, and she knew it wasn't going to be the last. She had to get over it and just do it because it wasn't going to get done if she didn't.

Charlotte opened the back of the van and grabbed two boxes of cupcakes. She knew they would help bring in cupcakes once she spoke to someone, but she didn't want to walk in without them. What if they didn't believe she was here to deliver cupcakes?

She walked toward the front door of the club and carefully juggled the two boxes in her left hand. She successfully opened the door and slipped into the club. Now to find someone to talk to and get all the cupcakes in here.

Charlotte walked past the empty reception area and into the littles' room. Technically, the club was opened to Littles and Daddies or Mommies right now, but most people were at work around this time, so they couldn't come.

If Charlotte had her way, she would never leave this room. She always felt comfortable in here, more comfortable than in her own home. Probably because Charlotte had to be an adult at her house, but here at the club, she could be herself, little and all.

Charlotte felt her shoe become looser, and she quickly looked down to see that it was untied. When she found someone to talk to about the cupcakes and set the boxes she had in her hand down, she would tie her shoe.

She knew she should've worn her Velcro shoes today, but she didn't want to feel little all day. Small things like Velcro shoes and certain clothes made Charlotte slip into little space a lot easier.

Charlotte didn't want that to happen at work since she had all of those cupcakes to decorate, but now she was regretting it.

"What can I do for you?" a deep voice asked.

Charlotte let out a little squeak and turned toward the voice quickly. Her right foot stepped on her shoelaces and threw her off balance.

Before Charlotte could react, she felt herself tumble forward, and she tried to catch herself, but it didn't work. Charlotte fell face down on the ground, cupcake and frosting spilling out of the boxes onto her and the floor.

She quickly looked up and toward the voice to see a man she didn't recognize. All Charlotte felt was mortification that she just tripped and fell in front of a person. How could she have done that?

Tears sprung to her eyes as she laid on the ground.

"Are you okay?" the man asked.

CHAPTER THIRTEEN

CHARLOTTE

t took a second for the pain to catch up to Charlotte, but once it did, she was a sobbing mess. The whole thing scared her, but there was also a lot of pain. Her body ached from falling onto the ground. She thought it was only going to be mortifying, but she should've known better.

She tripped really hard and hit the ground with no mercy. She knew there was going to be pain in the back of her mind, but she didn't really pay attention to it. There was a guy in front of her, and she just tripped.

So much happened in a short amount of time, and Charlotte didn't have enough time to process it all. All Charlotte wanted to do was hide in a corner away from anyone and everyone and cry in peace.

Out of the corner of Charlotte's eyes, she saw the guy's face turn into panic and rushed to her. The unknown man reached out toward Charlotte but took a step back when she shied away.

Charlotte didn't want to be touched by a man she didn't

know. Especially when she was hurt. All that went through her mind was that he could take advantage of her in this state. It was a fragile state, and she wanted someone she knew.

"Hey, it's okay," the guy said. "That was a nasty fall. Can I help you up?"

Charlotte whimpered and shook her head. She didn't want him near her, she wanted Finn.

"Daddy," she whimpered again, crying even louder than before.

She knew it wasn't right for her to call Finn Daddy, but she didn't care right now; she'd take the consequences later.

The man's eyes went wide, and he took a step back. "Who's your Daddy?"

"F-Finn," she cried out.

All she wanted to do was be held and comforted by him. She didn't know what she would do if he wasn't here.

The man's eyes went even wider. Charlotte watched as he brought his phone out and called someone, but she didn't fully register it.

The pain and shock were taking over, and she didn't want to have to think about anything. She just wanted to be held and cry.

Charlotte heard the man speaking on the phone but didn't pay attention to any of the words being said. His voice sounded urgent and rushed, which only fueled Charlotte to cry harder.

What was going on? Why was he speaking in a rushed tone? Who could he possibly be talking to?

Out of nowhere, Charlotte heard a door being slammed and heavy footsteps running toward them. Her heart rate picked up, and she looked over, trying to see who could possibly be coming over in such a rush.

Finn.

That was who, and Charlotte was so relieved he was here.

Finn quickly scooped Charlotte into his arms and rocked her back and forth.

"It's okay, my little cupcake," he murmured in her ear.

Charlotte cried harder in his embrace. The feeling of his arms wrapped around her made her feel safe and secure. She felt like she could let all her emotions out and be safe.

That Finn would keep her safe. She just knew he would, and she didn't have to worry about anything else.

"I bet it was so scary falling like that," Finn said. "I've got you now. It's going to be alright."

It was scary for Charlotte. It felt like she went down in slow motion, but at the same time, it happened so fast, and she couldn't catch herself.

"What happened?" Finn asked, and Charlotte knew it wasn't directed toward her but the other man in the room.

"She was walking in with the cupcakes we ordered when I asked her a question. She tripped on her untied shoelace," the man said.

Charlotte gasped at the mention of the cupcakes. She had cupcake frosting all over her, and she was getting it on Finn.

She tried to push away from Finn, but he wouldn't allow her.

"Shh. Stop wiggling, I don't want to drop you," Finn said.

"Messy!" Charlotte whined as she pushed up against Finn again.

"Oh hush," Finn said as he grabbed the back of her neck.

"I don't care if I get some frosting on my suit. All I care about is if you're hurt or not."

She stopped fussing for a second and stared into his eyes. He was telling the truth, but she still didn't feel right getting him all dirty.

"Now, you want to tell me what you were doing carrying cupcakes in here?" Finn asked. "Did you know your shoe was untied?"

Charlotte's eyes teared up again, and she shook her head. She didn't want to answer his questions because she knew she shouldn't have carried the two boxes of cupcakes in here. She knew she should have stopped and tied her shoe.

Charlotte knew she was in trouble and she didn't want to confess to anything. If James only had not asked her to do this, none of it would've happened. She could've avoided tripping and making a fool out of herself, but no, he had to ask her to deliver the cupcakes.

"No, you don't want to tell me why you were carrying the cupcakes, or no, you didn't know your shoe was untied?" he asked again.

Charlotte dug her head into his shoulder so she wouldn't be able to talk. She didn't want to face the disappointment or the punishment for answering the questions. She knew she was going to get punished for endangering herself.

Finn and Charlotte had been talking about rules if and when she became his baby girl. Charlotte still wasn't sure, but when they were talking about the rules, she longed to have them. She wanted to have guidelines and rules so she felt safe and secure.

Endangering herself was one of the rules. She wasn't supposed to endanger herself, and she did. She knew her shoe was untied, and yet she ignored it because she wanted to get the ball rolling on getting the cupcakes in here.

Charlotte knew she also shouldn't have carried in two boxes. James would've told her to go in and tell them the cupcakes were in the van for them to bring in. It wasn't his first preference for them to carry big boxes like that, but sometimes it had to be done.

She had thought since she and Amelia put the cupcake boxes in the van that it would be okay if she carried them into the club. She was wrong, and she wished she could go back in time and not bring them in.

She was now down twenty cupcakes, and she didn't know if she would be able to make them in time and have them delivered. She didn't even know if they needed them tonight or the next day.

"Charlotte," Finn warned her. "Answer the question."

The other man chuckled, and Charlotte realized that she had completely forgotten he was there. She let out a little squeal and dug her head into Finn's shoulder more. She couldn't believe she had been acting this way in front of a complete stranger.

"You've got your hands full with this little one," the man said.

Finn chuckled. "I do, but I wouldn't have it any other way."

If this wasn't such an awkward moment, Charlotte would have smiled, but she didn't. What did he mean Finn had his hands full? Was that a bad thing? Did she need to leave him alone?

"Sorry," Charlotte mumbled into his shoulder.

"What was that?" Finn asked.

"I'm sorry. I can leave so you can get back to work. I know you're busy," she whispered.

Charlotte hated to feel like she was bothering someone when they were busy, and right now, she felt that way. Finn was obviously busy, and she needed to not bother him.

She shouldn't have called out his name or called him Daddy. He wasn't her Daddy yet. She wasn't allowed to call him that, and yet she did.

There was so much guilt eating Charlotte up from the inside out. She knew better on a lot of things, yet she ignored them and decided to go ahead with them.

"Woah! Where did that come from?" Finn asked. "And don't think you're getting out of answering my questions from earlier."

Charlotte shook her head and pushed against his chest. She didn't have time to answer his questions. She needed to leave him alone and also get all of these cupcakes in here or else they would melt.

Her eyes went wide. "Cupcakes!" she screamed.

Finn flinched but held onto her. "What's wrong?"

"They're going to melt!"

"Don't worry. I've got people already getting them out of the van and putting them in the big refrigerators," the other man said.

"Thanks, Mac," Finn said.

Charlotte felt her shoulders relax a little at that. She was happy that she wasn't going to ruin any more cupcakes, but she was also disappointed that it couldn't be her to get them. She didn't want to be around Finn right now because she would have to answer his questions.

Questions she didn't want to ever answer.

"Before we have our talk, I want you to meet someone. This is one of the other owners of BTS. His name is Mac," Finn said as he pointed to the man.

Charlotte peeked over and took him in. He was tall like Finn but not as muscular. He had a beard and some tattoos peeking from under his sleeves.

"Hello, little one. I've heard all about you and am so glad I finally get to meet you!" Mac said, and he waved to her.

She shyly waved back before putting her face into Finn's neck again. Both of them chuckled, and Finn started to rub up and down her back.

"Can you clean this up while I go clean her up and have a talk with her?" Finn asked.

"Go ahead!" Mac said.

"Thanks. I owe you one."

Before Charlotte could process anything, Finn started walking toward the staircase he came from the other night. Where could he be taking her?

"I'm taking you to my office where we'll get you cleaned up and into new clothes before we have a talk," Finn explained as he walked up the stairs.

Charlotte thought about fighting this, but she knew it wouldn't do any good. She would just get into more trouble than she already was. Instead, Charlotte relaxed into his arms as he climbed the rest of the stairs.

She thought about asking him if he wanted her to walk since she wasn't the lightest person, but she stopped herself. Don't talk bad about herself. That was another rule Finn said she would have when and if she became his little girl.

That one was going to be hard for her since she did it all the time. She just felt like she always made mistakes and wasn't good enough. Something Finn said they would be working on.

Charlotte didn't tell him that, but he said he could just read it across her facial expression and her body language. Maybe she needed to take some classes to hide those.

"I don't have any girl clothes, but I do have some of my clothes here that you can wear," Finn said as he sat her down on the ground. "Let's get you cleaned off and into clean clothes."

Charlotte looked up at Finn and nodded her head. She knew if she didn't get cupcake frosting off of her that she would start to feel sticky and yucky. Not something she wanted right now.

"Can you walk into the bathroom and wash your hands while I get sweats and a shirt?" Finn asked and pointed to the bathroom.

Charlotte nodded her head again and made her way toward the bathroom. She silently washed her hands in the sink while she waited for Finn to come in. Thoughts ran through her head as she waited for him.

Would he be really mad at her for bringing in two big boxes of cupcakes instead of asking for help, or would he be more disappointed? Did he know that she knew about her untied shoelace and decided to ignore it until she talked to someone?

Charlotte didn't want to disappoint Finn, and she definitely didn't want him mad at her, but she seemed to be doing that a lot. He wasn't mad, but she could tell that he might have been annoyed when she didn't respond to him.

Maybe it wasn't a wise idea for her to say she was interested in him. She seemed to just be making him mad and disappointed, and Charlotte knew that it shouldn't happen all the time. Could she change something to help that, or would she need to let Finn know that she couldn't see this going any further?

"Ready to get changed? I don't think you had anymore frosting on you besides your hands," Finn said as he walked into the bathroom.

"Yes," Charlotte whispered, feeling timid all of the sudden.

Should she tell him now or wait until they start talking? Charlotte really wanted to get out of these clothes before she got into a serious conversation. She didn't want to be in nasty clothes for hours as they talked.

"Get changed, and then we'll talk," Finn said. He placed the clothes on the bathroom counter before he walked back out.

Charlotte slowly changed into his clothes. She tried to give herself enough time to think about things before she had to face Finn again. She thought it was best to just rip it off like a bandage and tell him first. Then maybe they wouldn't have to have the other conversation.

She timidly walked out of the bathroom and into Finn's office. He was sitting on the couch in front of his desk.

His head turned when he heard her walking, and he stood up.

"Are you ready to talk now?" Finn asked.

CHAPTER FOURTEEN

CHARLOTTE

*C*harlotte didn't know what to say. She wanted to tell him that no, she wasn't ready to talk and she wanted more time, but she knew it wasn't really a question. They were going to talk now, and she needed to be ready.

She nodded her head, but she knew that Finn could see how nervous and frightened she was to be talking to him.

"Take a couple deep breaths for me," Finn said, and Charlotte followed his directions.

Last time she took a couple deep breaths with Finn, it actually worked. She didn't think it would, but she surprisingly felt calm after.

This time, though, it didn't help much. Charlotte was still a ball of nerves. She just wanted to get this talk over with.

"Now, can you answer my two questions from before?" Finn asked.

Charlotte's mind went blank. She knew she was going to talk to him about something, but she couldn't remember the two questions he had asked downstairs.

She took a step back and looked down at her feet. Charlotte didn't want to make Finn even more mad for not remembering.

Charlotte had felt so overwhelmed with everything that she wasn't really processing much. Her breathing started to pick up as her heart rate increased.

"Charlotte," Finn said. "I need you to focus on my voice for me."

She tried her hardest to focus on his voice, but it was so hard. Charlotte just wanted to hide away in a corner and be left alone.

Hands grabbed hers and softly rubbed the back of her hand. It brought a little comfort in this high stress time.

"Charlotte, everything's gonna be okay. I bet it's been pretty overwhelming," Finn said. "I just want you to listen to my voice right now and try to calm down."

She nodded her head. His level of voice brought a little calmness down on her.

"Can you tell me what's wrong?" Finn asked.

Charlotte opened her mouth to speak but quickly shut it. Would he be mad at her?

Charlotte took the chance. "I-I d-don't remember the two questions."

"That's okay. I can repeat them for you," Finn replied. "The first one was why did you decide to bring in two cupcake boxes when there were people here to help?"

Charlotte thought about it for a second, not that she really needed the time because she knew the answer already.

"I wanted to be useful. It was only two boxes, and if my shoelace hadn't come untied, I wouldn't have fallen," Charlotte mumbled toward the end.

"Next time, only carry one or don't carry any at all.

Those boxes are huge, and a little girl shouldn't be carrying big things," Finn said.

Charlotte knew he meant well. He just wanted to make sure she was safe. She did know that she shouldn't have carried two boxes of cupcakes. She should've only carried one or none at all.

James would've said the same thing, and she knew it. It wouldn't be the first time James would've told her something like that. He had to constantly remind her that she shouldn't carry big things. Things that she couldn't see around or things that she could easily trip with.

Yes, Charlotte and Amelia did pack the car, but they carried one box at a time, so it was easier to see when they walked.

"I should've come in and asked for help," Charlotte said, not looking Finn in the eyes.

She didn't want to see the disappointment swirling in his eyes. It wasn't only that; his stare was intense, and she didn't think she could handle it right now.

"That's right. Next time, ask for help. There's no shame in asking for help. I ask all the time for someone to help me," Finn said.

"Otay," Charlotte whispered.

She didn't think she would forget this encounter the next time she had to deliver something. Hopefully she wouldn't have to deliver anything again, but she knew she would. James asked her to deliver things all the time. All the time was exaggerating, but Charlotte felt like it was all the time.

"Now, onto the second question. Did you know your shoelace was untied?" Finn asked.

Charlotte wanted to take a step back because she knew

the answer to the next question wasn't going to make him happy.

She opened her mouth, ready to say a lie.

"And before you think about lying, just know it's not good to lie. Lying gets you into trouble," Finn said before she could say anything.

Charlotte let out a sigh. "I did know," she whispered.

Silence. That's all Charlotte heard for what felt like several minutes, but she knew it was only a couple of seconds.

"Do I need to remind you about safety?" Finn asked.

Charlotte shook her head because she knew that it was dangerous. She knew she shouldn't have done it.

"Can you explain to me why you didn't tie them when you found out it came untied?" Finn asked.

She knew no matter what answer she gave, it wasn't going to be good enough. There was no excuse that was good enough for why she didn't tie her shoe.

"I wanted to find someone to talk to. There's no one at the front desk, and I didn't want the cupcakes to sit out for too long in the heat," Charlotte said. "I didn't think I was going to trip and fall until Mac said something to me. He scared me, and I flinched back."

She was hoping that maybe if she explained what happened that he wouldn't be disappointed or mad at her. Or, well, super disappointed and mad. She knew that he was already a little disappointed and mad for what she did.

James would be too, if he knew. Hopefully she didn't have to tell him what happened. She didn't need him fussing over her.

"Next time your shoe comes untied, stop immediately. Your safety comes first," Finn said.

"I didn't want to place the cupcakes on the ground. That would've been nasty and unsanitary," Charlotte tried to explain even more.

James had taught her only to put the baked goods on a counter or in the fridge. No where else.

So much for trying to obey James and his rules. Now she disobeyed Finn's rules. She didn't know which rules to go by anymore.

None of them were her Daddies, and she knew that, but that didn't help any. Charlotte knew that both of them wanted to keep her and the shop safe.

"I think it would've been okay for a couple of minutes since they were in a closed box," Finn said. "I just want you to be safe and not get hurt."

It warmed Charlotte's heart that he wanted that for her. Not many people in Charlotte's life had ever wanted her to be safe.

As Charlotte thought about that, tears sprang to her eyes. She didn't know how to deal with so many people caring about her all at once. Diana, James, and now Finn all cared about her.

"Why the tears?" Finn asked, a look of concern washing over his face.

Charlotte didn't want Finn to know that she had so few people who cared about her. She felt embarrassed by it because everyone else she knew had a whole family and more who cared about them. She just had three people, and none of them were blood related.

"Charlotte," Finn said as he cupped her face. "What's wrong?"

"I'm just really sorry," she sobbed out.

Finn wrapped his arms around Charlotte and held her against him. She felt safe and comforted in his arms. She never wanted to leave his embrace, but she knew she couldn't stay there forever.

"It's okay. You're okay now, and you know not to do it again," Finn said.

He pulled away from her and gave her a smile. She loved his smile, they always brightened up her day.

"I'm sorry I made a mess in front of someone. I didn't mean to embarrass you," she whispered, not looking into his eyes. "Sorry for also calling you Daddy without your consent. I know we've talked about me becoming your baby girl, but we haven't fully agreed on it yet. It wasn't okay for me to do that."

She felt bad about that. The guilt from calling him her Daddy was weighing down on her. She didn't know it at the time, but she loved it when she called him that. It felt so right, and she wanted to continue.

"Charlotte, can you lift your head for me?" Finn asked.

Charlotte closed her eyes and looked up. She didn't want to actually look at him, and he didn't say he had to. He just wanted her head to be lifted.

Finn chuckled. "I should've known you would do that. Can you please look at me?"

She shook her head. She didn't want to.

"Please. I want you to see how sincere I am. That I'm not mad at you," Finn said.

Charlotte thought about it for a second. He could be

trying to trick her and get her to open her eyes and make fun of her. But that didn't seem like Finn. He wouldn't do that to her.

She slowly opened her eyes and briefly glanced at him before looking away. He didn't look angry or ready to make fun of her, so Charlotte looked back at him.

"There you are," he whispered and gave her a smile.

She couldn't help but smile back at him. His smile was contagious, and he knew it.

"I'm not mad at you for making a mess in front of Mac. He's a Daddy Dom as well and was more worried about you than those cupcakes. I was worried more about you than those cupcakes. I could care less about them as long as you're alright," Finn said. "And as for you calling me Daddy. Well, we've talked about this, and while we aren't in a dynamic and you can't call me that, I'm okay with it. I know you need a little more time."

Charlotte took a breath of air and nodded her head. They had talked about it, but it still didn't give her the right to call him that.

"You were scared and called out the first thing that brought you comfort. It's okay, and I'm not mad at you," Finn said.

It still didn't make Charlotte feel better. What she did was wrong, and she shouldn't have done that.

"I can see the guilt in your eyes," Finn said. "How about this? You go stand in the corner and think about what you did. When I call you over, the punishment is over and all is forgiven."

Charlotte didn't like punishments, but deep down, she knew that this would help. That this punishment would take away the guilt that she felt for calling him Daddy when he wasn't hers.

She nodded her head, and Finn pointed toward the corner closest to his desk.

"Go stand there with your nose pointed up and your bottom sticking out," Finn instructed her.

Charlotte did as she was told and headed to the corner. She pointed her nose up and stuck her bottom out. It was an uncomfortable position, but punishments weren't supposed to be comfortable.

They were supposed to make her uncomfortable so she thought about the thing or things she did to get her here.

All Charlotte wanted to do was get through this punishment, get rid of all the guilt she felt for calling Finn Daddy when she wasn't supposed to.

It felt right to call him that. Charlotte felt comfortable around Finn, and she knew she wanted to get to know him more. She wanted to be his baby girl. Maybe she should tell him that soon, but she didn't know when.

Charlotte didn't think that this was the right time to tell him she wanted to be his baby girl, his sub. It just didn't feel right. She didn't want him to think that she was just saying that so she could call him Daddy after she accidentally did.

She didn't just want to call him Daddy. She wanted to submit to him, let him take care of her, cherish her, but also discipline her when she needed to. She wanted him for who he was because he was kind, compassionate, caring, but also could be hard at times when she needed discipline.

Finn made her feel safe and secure, loved, cherished, and so much more. She wanted that every day and not just when she saw him.

"You can come out now," Finn said.

Charlotte quickly turned around and ran toward him. His arms were stretched wide open, so she just crashed into his chest, but both of them didn't seem to care.

"All is forgiven," he whispered in her ear.

Charlotte relaxed against his embrace and just let him hold her. This is what she needed after standing in the corner for who knows how long.

"You're okay," he whispered again.

She pulled back from him, and he gave her a smile. She wanted to ask him if they could hang out the rest of the day together, but he probably had work.

Her eyes went wide at the thought of work. She should've been back at work a while ago.

"Work!" she managed to squeak out.

Finn's hands grabbed her shoulders so she couldn't move backwards.

"I already texted your boss saying you slipped and fell. He said for you to take the rest of the day off," Finn said.

Her shoulders sagged before they went stiff again. She couldn't claim PTO or sick days because she had already used up those days earlier in the year. James was now just paying her even though she wasn't at work, and that didn't sit well with her. Charlotte had tried to talk to James about it, but he didn't want to hear anything about it.

James kept telling her that it was something he could do for her since she worked so hard for him. Yes, she did work hard for him when she was there. She normally didn't take a break because they were always busy, and they didn't have any other baker.

Amelia could bake, but she didn't prefer to. She wanted

to be up in the front helping guests, and that was okay with Charlotte. Charlotte loved to bake, and she didn't like to be up front really. She didn't like talking to people, strangers specifically.

"Since we're already here, I wanted to talk about what we were going to talk about later today when we met up," Finn said. "Is that okay?"

Charlotte nodded her head. She knew he wanted to talk about something later today, but she didn't know what it was about.

"We're having a littles night tomorrow night. I know the club is already catered toward littles and their caregivers, but once or twice a year we do a celebration, a party. We bring in a bouncy house, cupcakes, food, people who paint faces, and other things," Finn explained.

Charlotte started to get excited. She had heard about these little parties that the club hosted, but she never went to one. She had joined a week or two after they had one a couple of years ago, and then Charlotte had to cancel her membership.

She had been dying to go to one but never had the money or time to go.

"Would you like to come and hang out with me and some other littles?" Finn asked.

Charlotte bounced up and down, clapping her hands.

"Yes!" she screamed.

She was so excited but quickly stopped when she realized she didn't have a membership anymore. How was she going to get in tomorrow night? She didn't have the money to pay for a one night access to the club nor did she have the money to start her membership again.

"Don't worry about the money or your membership. It's taken care of," Finn said.

Before Charlotte could answer, Finn's phone rang. He grabbed it from the desk and looked at who was calling him.

"Give me one second. I need to take this real quick," he said.

Charlotte watched as he stood up and walked over to the window of his office. She didn't realize that the window overlooked where the littles room was. Was that how he saw her the first night, or did he see her when he was coming downstairs?

Time had passed before Finn came back over. She didn't know how much time, and she didn't really care right now. All she cared about was that Finn was back.

"Do you want to hang out later this afternoon like we planned?" Finn asked.

Charlotte thought about it for a second. She wanted to hang out, but as she sat on the couch, she felt how tired she was. After a long day's work, the whole tripping ordeal, and the punishment, she was exhausted. Charlotte bet that if she laid down on the couch, she would be out like a light.

"I can see how exhausted you are. How about you just go home and get some rest?" Finn suggested.

She felt bad about having to cancel their hangout, but Charlotte was also glad she suggested she just go home. She really could use a nap after everything that happened today.

"I'll walk you to your car," Finn said before she could say anything.

Finn grabbed her hand and led her out of his office, through the club, and outside to the van. She was thankful he walked with her even though she knew the way back. It brought her peace and comfort.

"I'll see you tomorrow night?" Finn asked as he helped her into the van.

"Yes, sir," she whispered.

"Get home safely. Text me when you get there."

She nodded her head, and Finn shut the door. The drive back to the bakery wasn't long. Charlotte dropped off the keys with James before she made the short trek back to her house. By the time she got there, she was dead on her feet and ready to sleep.

Charlotte made a detour to her kitchen as her stomach grumbled, but all she found were several cans of beans and a half gallon of milk. None of it sounded appetizing, so she made her way to her bedroom and laid down, falling asleep right away.

CHAPTER FIFTEEN

FINN

A whole day had passed since Finn had last seen Charlotte. He didn't like going this long without seeing her, but right now, he couldn't do anything about it. Finn didn't want to push Charlotte into becoming his baby girl.

He could see every time they talked and hung out that she didn't want to leave, but he was waiting for Charlotte to say that. He was waiting for her to tell him that she wanted to be his baby girl.

Finn had mentioned it a couple of times, and each time, Charlotte said she needed to think about it. That it was a huge commitment, and she was right. It wasn't something he wanted her to just think about for thirty seconds and decide.

Granted, if she wanted to try being his baby girl and after a week realized that she didn't like it or him, she was free to leave. Would it hurt Finn to let her go? Absolutely, but he would do it.

Finn didn't want to force her into anything or keep her from leaving, even if it hurt a lot and went against everything in his body and mind. But he was hoping that once she said yes, she would realize how perfect they were together.

He had hoped that having her come to littles' night would show her that. Before they would walk into the big room, he wanted to ask her if, for tonight, they could try out being in the dynamic to see if she would even like it.

Finn so badly wanted to show her what it would be like to have him as a Daddy. If she said yes, tonight wouldn't show exactly how he would be, but it would give an idea. He had also thought about asking her if she wanted to come to his house for a weekend to see if she would like it and want to go from there. But he didn't want to overstep his boundaries. He had heard of some Doms pressuring subs into doing things for or with them, and he didn't want that. Finn didn't want to coerce her into anything, so he had kept a lot to himself.

He hoped that Charlotte would agree to tonight and be able to see if this was something that would interest her further. He knew she was a little, that was obvious, but he didn't know for sure if she was looking for a Daddy.

She hadn't told him that, and he didn't want to assume. All Charlotte told him was that she was interested in getting to know him more. That didn't give any insight on if she thought he was a potential Daddy or not.

For all Finn knew, Charlotte might just be looking for a boyfriend and not a Daddy. He didn't know if he could do that. Being a Daddy was in his bones, and only being a boyfriend would be hard. Half of himself would be missing from the relationship.

He really needed to get this cleared up before it was too late.

Finn had only seen Charlotte's little side twice so far.

The first time when she was in the club the night they met and the second time when she tripped and fell at the bakery. When they met, she was in little space longer, and when she tripped at work, she slipped into little space, but she didn't stay there long.

He couldn't blame her for pulling out of little space quickly. She was at work, and Finn didn't know if her boss knew she was little or not. He wanted to encourage her to continue to be in little space, but with her boss coming in, he didn't want to risk exposing her when she hadn't told him.

Finn wanted to see and interact with her more while she was little. He found that side of her adorable. Well, he found her adorable in any situation, but when she was little, it was precious.

Finn got up from his chair in his office and started to walk around. Charlotte had texted him this morning that she would get to the club herself and that he didn't need to pick her up.

He had insisted he pick her up so she didn't have to drive back after an exhausting but fun night, but she declined. Maybe she didn't want him to know where she lived. That was okay with him. Well, he wanted to know where she lived, so if something happened, he could go to her, but he understood why.

She was single, and he was a male. Finn was glad she told him no because that meant she was being safe. If that was her reasoning. Charlotte could honestly not want him to drive her because she wanted to be independent.

Finn didn't know, and he wouldn't know unless he asked. But he didn't know if he was going to ask; he probably wouldn't. He wanted tonight to be fun and enjoyable, not an interrogation. He could ask another day when it wasn't littles' night.

Finn's phone buzzed right as Mac walked into his office. The event was supposed to start soon, and he was hoping the notification was Charlotte telling him she was here.

But it wasn't.

CHARLOTTE

> I'm going to be running a couple of minutes late. I'll text you when I get there.

Finn let out a sigh and sat down on the couch. He was nervous about tonight, and he couldn't hide it. This night wasn't just catered toward Charlotte, but he wanted it to be special. He wanted to make her feel special.

"Why the sigh? Did Charlotte turn you down?" Mac asked as he sat down next to Finn. "How is she doing, by the way? Did she get hurt from the fall she took yesterday?"

Finn loved that Mac was worried and wanted to check up on Charlotte, but at the same time, he couldn't help but feel a little jealous. He knew Mac wouldn't do anything because he was already interested, and Mac could see that.

"Charlotte said she was going to be a little late. I'm just worried," Finn said.

This late in life, Finn knew not to bottle everything up. He could trust the other eight guys who owned and worked with him. They had all known each other for years and decided to do this together, and it worked.

It was a struggle in the beginning because all of them wanted to make it perfect and would go into someone else's lane and try to change things. They learned quickly that they were all good at something, and they stuck to their thing unless someone else approached them for help.

Ever since then, they'd worked well, and the club has been thriving. But through that whole process, Finn figured out not to bottle everything up but to confide in someone. It helped his stress levels, and it also made his life so much easier.

"Did she say she wasn't coming?" Mac asked.

Finn shook his head. "She said she would text me when she got here."

"There you go. She's coming, but she's going to be a couple of minutes late. She could've lost track of time picking out an outfit. You know how littles are when they are picking clothes out for themselves. It can take hours."

Finn groaned and nodded his head. That was very true. One time, they had a dress up party for the littles in the club, and it was mayhem. A lot of the littles didn't know what they wanted to wear, they threw clothes everywhere, and some littles even fought over clothes.

It wasn't pretty, and they'd never done a dress up party for the littles again. It took hours to clean up the mess, and half the clothes they had were torn or messy, and they had to throw them away.

"Should I call her and ask if she needs any help?" Finn asked Mac.

He was so unsure right now on what to do. He didn't want to overstep, but at the same time, he wanted to. Finn wanted Charlotte to know that he was there for her and she could come to him for anything.

"I would wait another ten to fifteen minutes. She could

be on her way right now, and you don't want to call her while she's driving," Mac suggested.

Finn relaxed into the couch as well as he could. He was worrying too much, and he knew that, but he couldn't do anything. He had tried taking several deep breaths in and let them out, but it didn't do much.

Until Charlotte was in the room, he wouldn't relax and stop worrying. He trusted Charlotte not to back out of things, that wasn't what was worrying him. He was worried that she may have a wreck, leave her house keys in her house, not charge her phone before she went out, not look around her surroundings as she walked to her car, and so much more.

He wanted to be there for her and help her out, watch over her so she didn't have to think about that.

Finn took a deep breath in. One step at a time. He had started to get to know her, and with each time they hung out, he could tell she liked him. It was only a matter of time before she asked him, and he wouldn't take any time to think.

He knew, and he was just waiting for her to be ready to become his baby girl.

"How is she doing after she fell?" Mac inquired.

"She's okay," Finn replied. "She was shaken up but no injuries."

"That's good. So you two are in a dynamic now?"

Finn let out a breath. He knew this was coming. Charlotte had told him that she called him Daddy before he got there and that was why she stood in the corner for fifteen minutes. To let her think about it and know that it was wrong since they weren't in a dynamic, but once the punishment was over, all was forgiven.

Finn was excited that she called him Daddy when she

was hurt. It showed that she trusted him and that she may want this, but he knew how she felt. Daddy was an honorific, and since they weren't in a dynamic, Charlotte shouldn't be calling him that. It was a respect thing, and at that moment, she hadn't thought about that.

He definitely wasn't angry at her when he found out. He understood that she was in shock and hurt and might have regressed and called out the first thing she wanted. Her Daddy, which she then said was him.

"We aren't technically in one right now. We've talked to each other about getting into one, but we haven't actually said we are," Finn said, and he looked over at Mac.

He wanted to see his reaction to this. Mac was a Dom who stuck to the rules all the time.

"Oh," he said. "I just thought since she called you Daddy that you guys were in a dynamic."

Finn had a feeling that Mac wanted to say more but was holding it in. He probably wanted Finn to explain before he said anything else, and Finn respected him for that. A ton of people would have given their opinions before they got the whole story but not Mac. He always waited until he got the whole story before he said anything.

"We weren't in a dynamic when that happened. She felt guilty about it and told me, so I punished her. She stood in the corner for fifteen minutes," Finn explained.

"Good," Mac said.

Finn chuckled and shook his head. He knew that coming because Mac was all for rules and following them. He was definitely a strict Daddy, and there was nothing wrong with that. Whoever his little girl ended up being would be lucky to have him as a Daddy.

Mac really cared about anyone, and he showed that by being strict and having rules.

"So what are you going to do about it?" Mac asked.

"I don't know," Finn replied. "I really don't know. I want to ask her to become my baby girl, my sub, but I don't want to push her. I'm nervous that if I ask, I may run her off."

"So talk to her about that and bring it all up. Communication is key."

Finn nodded his head. Communication was key, and he hadn't been doing a good job of that. It was something he was always working on and could only improve on.

"I have faith that you'll do the right thing. You'll figure it out," Mac said as he stood up from the couch. "I'll see you down there when Charlotte comes."

Finn relaxed on the couch as he waited for Charlotte to text him. He couldn't wait until she got here. Now to just wait for her.

CHAPTER SIXTEEN

CHARLOTTE

*N*erves ran through Charlotte's body as she got closer to the time when she needed to leave for the club. This was going to be the first time Charlotte went to the club without Diana.

Even when Charlotte had a membership, Diana would always drive her there and make sure everything was okay. It was new to go by herself, and Charlotte didn't know if she liked it or not.

She did know Finn, but this was different than before. Diana was a friend, and there was nothing romantically going on, but with Finn, it was a lot different.

He was a potential Daddy, someone she really wanted to be in a dynamic with, and she didn't want to mess up. Charlotte had suspected that she was young in age when she slipped into little space, but she hadn't actually tested it out yet. She didn't want to go that young and not have anyone there in case something happened.

It scared her, and now she was in a predicament. What if she fell so far into little space that she had an accident? She didn't own any diapers or Pull-Ups, not that she would wear one tonight anyways.

Charlotte knew it would be hard to change herself, especially if she was feeling that little. She didn't want to take any chances and get a rash when it could have been prevented.

She didn't want to scare Finn off. What if he didn't want a little that young? Charlotte really liked him, but she didn't know if she would be able to be with him if he didn't want her for who she was.

Charlotte was also excited to go tonight because it would be her first big littles' event at the club. She couldn't wait to meet some of the other littles and make friends with them.

She had hoped once she got more money and could renew her membership that she could continue to see those friends she made and also have a safe play to be little. Charlotte didn't have a lot of friends, and she wanted more.

She wasn't very social, but that was okay. The friends she would make would be enough. Ten seconds of courage was all Charlotte needed to go up to a little and ask to color or play with them. It seemed so daunting, and she wasn't even at the club yet.

Charlotte looked at the clock, and her eyes went wide. She was going to be late if she didn't leave now, and she didn't want that. She rushed to the door, grabbed her keys, and opened the front door.

Envelopes on the ground caught her attention, and she stopped. Charlotte picked them up and walked to her car. She didn't use her car much because she didn't like to drive, but she wanted to be a little independent tonight before she was little and depended on Finn and the other monitors in the room.

Charlotte didn't like her independence, but she wanted to show Finn that even if they got into a dynamic that he wouldn't have to care for her twenty-four seven. She didn't want to exhaust him or run him away.

She didn't know if he wanted to be in a twenty-four seven dynamic or just when they were together, so Charlotte picked just when they were together. It was safer, so in case he didn't want the twenty-four seven dynamic, she wouldn't get hurt or displease him.

Charlotte had never cared this much about how she should act, but she wanted this to work between them.

She sat in her car and looked at the envelopes real quick. Electric and water were in bold on the envelopes, and her heart leapt in her chest, not in a good way. Charlotte knew she was behind on payments for her water and electric bill, and getting mail on them wasn't good.

Charlotte carefully opened the envelopes and pulled out the pieces of paper. She scanned the documents and saw in big bold letters on both of them that if she didn't pay her electric and water bill in two weeks, they would shut it off.

Worry filled Charlotte at the thought of her utilities being shut off. She didn't do well in the dark, and she knew if the electricity got cut off, night time would be terrible. Charlotte slept with a night-light in every night.

Charlotte pulled out her phone and quickly sent a text to Finn.

CHARLOTTE

I'm going to be running a couple of minutes late. I'll text you when I get there.

She didn't like to be late to things, but she needed to wrap her mind around this before she walked into the club. Charlotte didn't want to worry about anything tonight, including this new information she got.

Finn was very good at telling when something was off, and she didn't want to ruin the mood. She wanted to be free and not have to worry about adult life for a little bit, and she didn't want Finn to worry about her.

Charlotte had already been looking into a second job on her evenings since she didn't work at the bakery. She had gotten hired at the cafe that Finn and her went to the other day. It wasn't ideal, but Charlotte had to do what she had to do to pay the bills.

She started work at the cafe in the next couple of days, and she hoped she would be able to earn enough money and get paid to pay the bills on time. Charlotte highly doubted that she could, but she needed to try. She didn't want to give up yet.

James, Amelia, and Finn didn't know that she had gotten a second job, and she wasn't going to tell them. Her time with Finn would have to decrease, but it was a sacrifice Charlotte was willing to make. Well, not willing but that she had to make.

It was going to be hard in the beginning, but once Charlotte had saved up some money, then she could work a little less and spend more time with Finn.

She felt guilty for keeping the secret, but they didn't need to know right now. It wasn't important, and they hadn't asked. Just like she wanted right now.

Charlotte took a couple deep breaths in and let them out slowly. She remembered what Finn had told her when he got anxious or nervous about things, take a couple deep breaths and let them out. It had worked the previous day when she got nervous, and it was working now.

She turned the car on and drove to the club. The whole way there, Charlotte felt nervous about tonight. What would it be like? Would she make any friends? Would she embarrass herself or Finn?

Charlotte turned the car off and sat in the parking lot for a couple of minutes. It was darker outside, and Charlotte didn't want to walk to the front door by herself. She had told Finn she would text him when she got to the club, but she wasn't feeling brave right now.

All her braveness was going toward being inside the club, and she was stuck inside of her car right now. With shaky hands, Charlotte texted Finn.

CHARLOTTE

I'm outside in the parking lot, front row. Can you come to me?

It took her several seconds to actually send the text, but once she did, she was relieved. She wouldn't have to walk alone in the dark tonight.

Charlotte knew that was why working at the bakery was so appealing. She loved baking, but she also got out before it even started to get dark, so if she had to walk home, she could in the daylight. It was a win-win in her eyes.

Now she just needed to be brave or drive herself when she worked at the cafe. She knew she wouldn't be able to walk home every night when she worked at the cafe. It was already exhausting suppressing her little side all day and night, and she didn't need the added stress of walking home at night. But she also didn't need the extra stress of driving to and from work.

Charlotte didn't know what to do, but she was going to have to figure it out soon. Her first shift at the cafe was in two days.

A knock sounded on Charlotte's car window, and she jumped in her seat, wide eyes as she stared into Finn's. She turned the car off and got out of the car.

"Hello, little one. Drive here safely?" Finn asked.

He wrapped his arms around her and held her close to him for several seconds. She melted into his arms and found herself leaning into him. Charlotte loved it when he called her little one, but she also loved it when he hugged her.

Safe and secure.

That's what Charlotte felt every time he wrapped his arms around her. Something she hadn't felt in years and cherished every time it happened.

"I did," she whispered.

Charlotte didn't know if that was a lie or not. She didn't remember any of the drive here, too worried about tonight and the bills she had to pay.

"Are you excited for tonight?" he asked as they walked toward the front entrance.

Charlotte felt her hands start to shake. "Yes." Her voice was shaky.

She hung her head and tried to hide from Finn. She didn't want him to know that she was so nervous about tonight. Charlotte didn't want him to know that while she was excited, her anxiousness was higher than normal.

Finn stopped and cupped her face with his hands. They

made eye contact, and Charlotte couldn't look away, no matter how intimidating his stare was.

"What's wrong?" he asked.

Before Charlotte knew what was happening, tears sprang to her eyes. She tried to blink several times to get rid of them, but it wasn't working. All the anxiousness bottled up inside of her was overfilling and spilling out.

"Oh, little one. Tell me what's wrong." Finn wiped away the tears as they slid down her face.

Charlotte opened her mouth to tell him, but a sob came out. So much had happened in the past several hours, and it was all coming out. All day Charlotte had felt the anxiousness inside of her, and she didn't do anything about it. She didn't know what to do.

James had seen that something was wrong and asked her multiple times if she was alright or needed anything. Charlotte didn't want to tell him anything, and so she lied and said she was okay.

Charlotte didn't like lying to anyone.

"It's okay. Take a couple of deep breaths in for me," Finn instructed as they stood outside the front door.

Charlotte was worried that someone would see them out front, but Finn made sure she was focused on him and only him.

"Listen to my voice as you take several deep breaths in. Just focus on me," he said.

She did exactly what he instructed and took several deep breaths in. Charlotte felt herself calm down after a little while.

"Now, can you tell me what's got you so worked up?" Finn asked.

"I'm just nervous," Charlotte whispered.

She didn't know how he was going to react. Would he be understanding that she was nervous, or would he tell her to grow up?

"It's okay to be nervous about tonight. It's a big night, and so many littles in there are nervous, but you'll make a lot of friends and be comfortable in no time," he said. "I had wanted to talk to you before you walked in. I was wondering if you would like to be my baby girl tonight to see how it would feel. If you don't want to, that's okay, but if you do, I would love it."

Charlotte was shocked. He knew the right things to say at the right time. She also didn't know how to feel about him wanting to be her Daddy tonight. She was excited that he proposed that, but she was also nervous again about it.

"You know the rules we talked about a couple of days ago? The rules that I would give my baby girl," Finn asked, and Charlotte nodded her head. "Those are the rules you would have to follow tonight."

She felt herself nodding her head again. The rules weren't bad, and they made her feel safe. Charlotte had found herself following them as closely as she could in the day, but she didn't know how well she was doing about that. She didn't have anyone to correct her.

"You would rely on me, and I would take care of you tonight. If it's something you're interested in, we can do it, but if it's not, then we won't," Finn said.

Charlotte found herself thinking about it for a second. It sounded like a good idea because people would be around them, and if anything happened, they would be there to stop it or take her away from him. It would give her a taste of what he was like as a Daddy, and that excited her.

"So what do you think?" Finn asked.

She nodded her head, and he gave her a disapproving look.

"Words, little girl," he said.

She blushed and looked down at her feet. It would be the second time she called him Daddy, but this time it would be alright since they agreed to things.

"Yes," she whispered. She chickened out of calling him Daddy.

"Yes what?" he asked.

Charlotte looked at Finn. "Yes, Daddy."

She felt all tingly inside and couldn't help herself from smiling. It felt amazing to call him Daddy, and she loved every second of it. Apparently, he felt the same way because a huge grin spread across his face.

"Now, are you ready to have some fun?" Finn asked.

Charlotte gave him a great big smile. "Yes!"

They walked in, hand in hand, past the receptionist and into the littles room. A gasp escaped past her lips as she took everything in.

It was perfect.

CHAPTER SEVENTEEN

CHARLOTTE

he cupcakes Charlotte had made were nicely displayed across two tables. There were several spots on the table that had missing cupcakes, and she saw littles and caregivers eating them.

Joy filled her heart as she saw all the happy faces eating the cupcakes.

"The cupcakes have been a hit," Finn said.

His hand was on the lower part of her back as he guided her through the club. Charlotte couldn't take her eyes off of everything. There was a bouncy house; coloring section, face painted station, and more.

Heaven. Absolute heaven.

Charlotte wanted to go and do everything, but she didn't know where to start. If she started with the bouncy house, then the coloring station would be left all alone, and she didn't want that.

She wished she could do all of them at once, but she knew it wasn't possible.

"Charlie," Finn said. "You can go play. I'll be right here."

Charlotte stared at him with wide eyes before she looked all around her. She didn't know what she wanted to do at first. There were too many options, and she knew she was starting to feel overwhelmed with it all.

"Charlie?" Finn asked.

She looked back at Finn and blinked several times. What did he want?

"Are you okay?" He grabbed her hand and brought her close to him. "Remember you can tell me anything. No secrets between Daddy and his baby girl."

Charlotte took a deep breath in. If she wanted this to work between them, she needed to be honest.

"There's so many options," she whispered. "I-I don't know what to do first."

Her eyes welled up with tears again, and Finn brought her into his arms.

"It's okay. How about I pick for you so you don't have to," Finn suggested. "If you go and do it and it isn't fun, then come back to me, and we'll find something."

She nodded her head and waited for him to tell her which one to do. Charlotte looked all around the room, but her eyes kept going back to the coloring section. She had always loved coloring, and that was how Finn and her had met.

"How about you go and color with that girl. I bet she needs a friend." Finn pointed over at the coloring section.

There were a few littles coloring there, but they were all together while this one girl was by herself. Charlotte looked up at her Daddy before she looked at the girl again.

She didn't want to leave him, but she also wanted to go color.

Finn patted her bottom and gave her an encouraging smile. "I'll be right here the whole time if you need me."

That was all Charlotte needed to skip over toward the girl. She grabbed a coloring book and some markers and plopped herself down next to the girl. Charlotte didn't know what came over her, but it was like she was a new person. Before, she would have never gone up to the girl and sat down next to her.

"Hi! I'm Charlie, well, Charlotte is my full name," she said as she started to color.

"I'm Jane, but people call me Janie," she introduced herself.

Charlotte didn't know what to do next. Did they sit in silence and color together? Did they talk to each other and get to know each other and become friends? Did Janie even want to become friends with her?

"What are you coloring?" Janie asked her.

Charlotte pointed at the cupcake she was coloring. "Cupcakes! They are the best thing ever! As well as any baked goods."

Janie's face lit up. "I loooove baked goods! Especially the sweet ones. The sugar high you get and the deliciousness you get with each bite you take."

Both of the girls sighed in content at the thought of eating baked goods. Charlotte realized that was something that they had in common.

"You should come over to Heavenly Baked bakery soon! I work there," Charlotte suggested.

"I've wanted to go there for a while but have been too nervous to go in," Janie said. "I'll have to come in soon!"

Janie and Charlotte colored their pictures in silence for a

couple of minutes. Charlotte didn't feel like they needed to talk all the time, and she liked that.

"What's your favorite color to color with?" Charlotte asked Janie.

She had seen her color with the blue primarily but didn't want to make any assumptions.

"Pink!" Janie enthusiastically said. "I love any shade of pink! What about you?"

Charlotte thought about it for a second. She liked red, but it wasn't her favorite color.

"I really like baby blue. I guess with my hair being red and Christmas being blue and red, and green in there, it just became my favorite color," Charlotte explained. "I love Christmas! It's the best time of the year."

Janie nodded her head, but Charlotte could tell Christmas wasn't her favorite time of the year, and that was okay. Charlotte knew that not everyone liked Christmas. Some people were sad around that time because they didn't have any family, but it didn't mean she couldn't love it any less.

"My favorite holiday has to be Easter." Janie perked up. "I love hunting for the plastic eggs and getting little presents!"

Charlotte agreed with her. Easter was a good holiday, and she couldn't wait for Easter to come around. It was a good holiday, and all the colors made it so pretty.

They went back to coloring their pictures. Charlotte was glad she met Janie and they became friends. She hoped they could stay friends for a long time. Maybe they could even have playdates later on.

That would be so much fun! Right as Charlotte was going to ask Janie, she spoke.

"Do you have a Daddy here?" Janie asked as she looked at Charlotte.

Charlotte shrugged her shoulders. "It's complicated."

Janie sat up straight and stopped coloring. "Tell me."

She wanted to open her mouth and tell Janie all about it but didn't know if Finn would like that. Charlotte looked over at Finn, who was talking to a man she didn't recognize, but he was looking at her.

Finn waved his hand and gave her a smile.

"That's your Daddy? Finn?" Janie asked.

"Well, promise you won't tell anyone?" Charlotte looked at Janie.

She hadn't been able to talk to anyone about this besides her stuffie. She didn't feel comfortable talking to Diana, James, or Amelia about this, and Charlie wanted to talk to someone about it.

"I promise!" Janie raised her voice in excitement.

Charlotte took a deep breath. "I met him over a week ago here at the club. He came up to me and wanted to color while I did. We got to know each other, and we've talked about him being my Daddy, but nothing has happened."

"Well, what's wrong?"

Charlotte felt silly saying this. "He'll be my first Daddy, and I'm nervous. What if I make so many mistakes and he doesn't want me anymore?"

Arms wrapped around her, and Charlotte found herself laid out across the ground.

"Be yourself! He'll love you for you and no one else," Janie said, her arms still wrapped around her.

Charlotte nodded her head because that was what she had told herself several times but psyched herself out and told herself that she needed to be perfect.

Janie didn't let go of Charlotte, so she wrapped her arms around her, and they hugged. She'd never had another little give her a hug out of the blue, and she kind of liked it. It was unexpected, but it was nice.

"Charlie?" Finn's voice rang out. "Are you okay?"

Janie got off of Charlotte, and they both turned toward him, but he wasn't alone. Standing with him was an unknown man and Mac. Charlotte saw Janie's face turn red as she looked down at her lap.

Mac was intensely staring at Janie. Could something be going on between both of them? Was that her Daddy?

Charlotte leaned closer to Janie and whispered, "Mac is looking at you. Is he your Daddy?"

Janie's eyes went wide, and she shook her head. Charlotte looked between both of them and knew something was going on. Did Janie know that something was going on?

"Charlie?" Finn called out her name again.

She looked over at Finn and gave him a smile. "Everything's fine! We were talking about cupcakes and other baked goods!"

Finn chuckled. "Do you want a snack or anything to drink?"

Charlotte thought about it a second. She wanted a drink, but she didn't want to leave Janie here by herself. They had become friends, and she didn't want her to be alone.

"I've got to go. I'm needed at home," Janie softly said.

Charlotte let out a little whine but hugged Janie.

"We need to get together!" Charlotte said. "Come by the bakery!"

"I will!" Janie said before she started to walk away.

Mac followed after her, and it was just the unknown man, Finn, and Charlotte.

"Charlie, can you answer my question?" Finn asked.

"Both?" She looked up at him.

Both of the men chuckled, and Finn helped Charlotte off the ground. All three of them walked to the bar, Finn helping Charlotte up on one of the seats.

"I would like you to meet my friend and other owner of the club, Jaxson," Finn said.

Charlotte got shy and looked down at her hands. She didn't really enjoy meeting new people.

"Charlie," Finn warned her. "It's not nice to ignore people."

Charlotte looked up and made eye contact with Jaxson.

"Hi," she whispered.

"Hello, little one. It's so nice to meet you. Finn has told me so much about you," Jaxson said.

"Dadddyyy," Charlotte whined. "No talking about me."

What if Daddy had said something bad about her? Would Jaxson think less about her?

"Charlie, we don't whine. I didn't say anything bad about you, so hush," Finn said as he placed some crackers and a juice box in front of Charlotte.

Charlotte loved that she could call Finn her Daddy right now. It felt so right and comforting. He would take care of her tonight, and she didn't have to worry about it.

"Eat and drink up," Finn said. "Jaxson and I have known

each other since we were little kids. If you need anything and can't get a hold of me, ask for him."

She nodded her head and happily sipped on her juice. She didn't really understand why Daddy was telling her this, but she stored it away in her brain for later. Nothing would ever happen to her or him.

"Do you understand?" Finn asked. "Charlie, I need you to look at me and tell me you understand."

Charlotte let out a sigh, placed her juice box on the table, and turned toward him.

"Yes, Daddy. I understand," Charlotte murmured.

Jaxson chuckled to himself. "You've got your hands full with this little."

"I do, but I wouldn't have it any other way."

Charlotte finished up her crackers and juice. She happily started to swing her legs back and forth and looked around the room.

"Do you want to go jump in the bouncy house?" Finn asked.

She shook her head. Charlotte didn't want to leave Finn right now. Everything looked fun, but she didn't want to go and meet new people. All the confidence she had before went away as she sat with Jaxson and her Daddy.

"Do you want to go and get your face painted?" he asked.

"No, I'm otay here," she whispered.

"Okay. Do you want another juice box?"

Charlotte nodded her head quickly and made grabby hands. Both men smiled, and Finn handed her another juice box. She happily drank while Jaxson and Finn talked.

"She's so cute," Jaxson said.

"She really is." Finn looked at Charlotte.

Time had passed as Jaxson and Finn talked, Charlotte happily swinging her legs and drinking juice. She started feeling her eyes droop, and she knew she needed to go to bed. Tomorrow morning was going to be a killer if she didn't.

"Dadddyyy," Charlotte whispered loudly.

"Yes, Charlie?" Finn looked at her.

"Come cwoser." She beckoned him toward her.

Finn looked at Jaxson before he leaned closer to Charlotte.

"I is tired," she whined. "Sweepy."

Finn stood to his whole height and looked at Jaxson. "Could you drive her car home while I drive her in mine?"

"Sure thing. I've got nothing better to do. We're over-staffed anyways, so two of us leaving won't matter," Jaxson said.

Finn turned back toward Charlotte and bent down to her height.

"I'm going to drive you home, and Jaxson is going to drive your car," he said.

Charlotte went to protest, but Finn placed his hands on her mouth before she could.

"You're really tired and little right now. Little girls don't drive." He grabbed her hand.

Finn led her out of the club and to his car after he gave Charlotte's keys to Jaxson. It took a little while for Finn to get Charlotte's address out of her, but once she was happily situated in his car, she complied.

"I sweep," she whispered.

"No, no, no," Finn said. "You need to stay awake for me, baby girl. Play with my fingers to stay awake."

Finn placed his hand in hers as he drove, but Charlotte didn't grab his right away.

"Charlie," Finn sang her name.

She looked over at him and grabbed his hand. Charlotte just wanted to sleep, but deep down, she knew that she needed to stay awake. Daddy had asked her to, and she was trying her hardest to.

"We're almost there," he said.

"Sleeeeeep!" Charlotte whined.

"We're here. Can I have your keys to help you get inside?" Finn asked.

That pulled Charlotte right out of being little. She didn't want him to see her place. It was a mess, and she had a couple other bills that were overdo on her kitchen table. She didn't want him to see those at all.

"It's okay. I've got it from here," Charlotte mumbled.

"I'm really fine walking you in and tucking you into bed," he said.

"I've got it." She took a deep breath in. "I-I'm not ready for you to see inside yet."

Finn nodded his head. "That's okay. Text me when you go to bed. I'll stay out here until you go inside."

Charlotte unbuckled herself and got out of the car. She turned around and looked at Finn.

"Thank you. I really enjoyed tonight," she whispered.

"I really enjoyed tonight as well. I'll see you later?" he asked.

Charlotte nodded her head and walked away from the car. She didn't bother to close the door because Jaxson was walking up to her.

"Here's your keys," he said as he handed them to her. "Have a good night."

"You too," she said.

Charlotte walked to her front door and unlocked it. She turned around and waved to Finn before she walked into her messy house. She really needed to clean her house.

She let out a sigh and walked to her room, brushed her teeth, and got into bed.

CHARLOTTE

Goodnight

Charlotte set her alarm, plugged her phone in before she closed her eyes, and fell asleep.

CHAPTER EIGHTEEN

CHARLOTTE

*C*harlotte had woken up in a panic. She had slept through her alarm and was late for work. Or, well, that was what she woke up and thought. She had completely forgotten that today was her day off. Her day off from the bakery and her last day before she started her new job.

Charlotte knew what she had to do on her day off, but she didn't want to. She needed to clean her house, see if she could sell anything that she didn't use, and try to get some good sleep before working two jobs.

She also had Finn on her mind. Since last night, Charlotte had him constantly on her mind. She wanted to become his baby girl, and she thought she might tell him that today. It was something she had given thought to, and she loved it last night.

She didn't know where she was going to sell things, if she could even find anything to sell. Charlotte wasn't good with these things, and she knew it. She didn't want to part with anything in her house because everything had a meaning to it.

Well, almost everything had a meaning to it. The stuff she had bought while she was in little space wasn't as meaningful. They were mostly stuffies, and she couldn't sell them. They would be all alone out in the world when they could stay with her.

Maybe it was time for Charlotte to make hard decisions and get rid of some of them that she couldn't have anymore. Find them new homes with other littles or little kids. An idea popped into her head.

The club had a little shop where they take stuffies that littles don't want anymore, pay them a little money, and then sell it to other littles who want them. She could take some of them and give it to the club so other littles there could find their stuffies.

It would break Charlotte's heart to give them to the club, but she didn't know what else to do. She had gotten rid of her cable and unplugged her TV so she wouldn't be able to turn it on and get the basic channels.

She was also hoping that it would help cut down on the cost of her electric bill. Charlotte was hoping and praying for that because she didn't know what else to do.

Charlotte was bad at managing things and seeing where money was going. She knew once she started to work her second job that she would be busy and too tired when she got home. She didn't look forward to that.

She got up from her seat at the table and went over to her spare room where she kept all of her stuffies. It was her playroom when she wanted somewhere 'safe' to go. Charlotte knew that her whole house was safe, but there was something about having one room that made it special and feel extra safe.

The room was full of stuffies when Charlotte walked in. Her heart had already started to break, but as she looked at them, her heart broke even more.

Charlotte slowly went through all of them, and she put several in a corner to give to the club. She didn't get rid of a lot, but this was a start for her. Maybe in a couple of days she could find more to give to the club and earn some money. Charlotte knew every penny counted right now.

She sighed, grabbed the trash bag, and stuffed all the stuffies into it. Charlotte didn't want to see them as she drove to the club. She knew if she saw them looking at her she wouldn't be able to bring them in.

Her keys laid on the counter next to her wallet. She took a deep breath and grabbed them as she walked toward the front door.

Charlotte's heart broke more with each step she took toward her car. She threw them into the back, got in, and started the car. Charlotte took several deep breaths, and her eyes started to water. She didn't want to do this.

The drive to the club was short, and Charlotte wished it lasted a little longer. She got out of the car, grabbed the bag full of stuffies, and dragged her feet to the entrance of the club.

She sniffled and opened the door to the club, stepped in, and walked to the shop to drop them off.

"Can I help you?" a man asked behind a desk.

Charlotte didn't look up from the ground. She didn't want him to see the tears in her eyes. She took in a shaky breath of air and blinked several times.

"I-I'm here to g-give my stuffies," Charlotte whispered.

"Okay. Can I have a look at those?" the person asked.

Charlotte held up the trash bag for the guy but didn't look up. She didn't want to see the man pulling out her stuffies.

"Can I ask why you're getting rid of these?" the man asked. "Is someone forcing you?"

Charlotte shook her head because no one was forcing her to get rid of them but herself.

"Can you look at me and tell me?" he asked again.

She blinked several times and took a couple of deep breaths before she looked up at the man. He was giving her a sad smile, and her eyes started to water again.

"It's okay to cry," the man said. "Can you answer my two questions?"

"N-no one is f-forcing me to get rid of them. I n-need some money, and I've got a lot of stuffies," Charlotte whispered toward the end.

The man had started to take her stuffies out of the garbage bag, and she had to look away. Charlotte needed to stop calling them *her* stuffies in her head because they weren't anymore. They were the club's until someone bought it.

Oh, how she was going to miss those stuffies.

"What's your name?" the man asked.

"Charlotte," she said.

"Well, Charlotte. My name is Jonah, and these stuffies are just wonderful. So many littles are going to love these," Jonah said.

That didn't help Charlotte at all. She didn't want to get rid of them, and he said all the wrong things. He was supposed to tell her that she didn't need to get rid of them, but he didn't.

"Oh, honey, it's going to be okay," he said. "I know you'll miss them, but it's going to be okay."

Tears fell down Charlotte's face the longer Jonah talked.

"Charlotte?" another person said, and she instantly recognized the voice as Mac.

She quickly turned around and looked to see if Finn was around. She didn't want him to see her right now. He couldn't know that she was struggling for money or that she was crying over stuffies.

Mac's face turned serious when he looked at her face. He quickly walked over to her and bent down in front of her.

"Are you okay? Why are you crying? Did you fall again?" Mac fired off.

Before she could answer, Jonah answered behind her.

"She didn't fall, but she did bring stuffed toys in. The littles are going to be so happy when they see we have new stuffed toys for them," Jonah said. "I can give you seventy-five dollars for all of these."

Charlotte sniffled and looked down at her feet. Her heart broke even more when he told her the price. She didn't want to give them up, but seventy-five dollars would help some toward her bills. She needed the money, and it meant she had to make sacrifices right now.

"Charlotte, can you look at me?" Mac asked.

She shook her head and turned around. She didn't need to talk to him right now. All she wanted to do was take the cash and leave.

Before she could grab the money Jonah was holding out for her, her body stilled.

"Charlie?" Finn asked.

How did he know she was here? She didn't tell him that today was her day off and that she was here.

"Charlie, you can't ignore me," he said again.

She hated that he called her that right now. Him calling her Charlie made her want to run into his arms and tell him everything that was going wrong. She wanted him to take care of her.

Charlotte slowly turned around and looked at Finn who stood right next to Mac. Did Mac tell him that she was here?

"Mac texted me and said you were crying in the shop. What's wrong, little one?" Finn asked.

She shook her head. She didn't want to tell him anything, but the look he gave her made her rethink it. He wasn't her Daddy yet, but he still had an effect on her.

"I was selling some of my s-stuffies to the club," she softly spoke.

She was hoping he wouldn't have her repeat it because Charlotte knew if she did, she would break down.

"Why?" he asked.

"I d-don't need them anymore." She looked everywhere but in his eyes.

"Here's your money," Jonah said again.

Charlotte turned around and grabbed the money, not looking at what used to be her stuffies at all. She watched as Finn walked over to Jonah and whispered something in his ear, Finn's eyes on Charlotte the whole time.

She felt uncomfortable and started to walk toward the exit of the club. Right now, Charlotte just wanted to go home and lay in her bed. She didn't want to do anything but mope around because she had just lost a couple stuffies.

"Don't you dare walk outside this club," Finn said.

Charlotte immediately stopped walking. She wasn't going to leave without saying goodbye to him first. Well, she might have left if she felt like she was going to break at any moment and burst into tears.

"I'll see you later," Mac said. "It was nice seeing you, Charlotte."

Finn grabbed her hand and turned her around.

"See you, Mac," he said before he turned back to Charlotte. "Can we talk?"

Charlotte nodded her head because she did want to talk to him. She wanted to bring up them trying out being in a dynamic together, him being her Daddy. She had thought about it all morning as she went through her stuffies, and she was sure she wanted this.

"I—" she cleared her throat. "I wanted to talk to you about something."

"We can talk in my office, or we can talk in the little coffee room we have," Finn said.

"Coffee room?"

Charlotte could use some coffee right now. She started to feel her body getting tired after crying for a while. Finn led her to the room and pulled out a seat for her.

"How do you like your coffee?" he asked. "Don't get used to drinking coffee. I would normally say no, but I think you could use it after that hard moment."

She was grateful that he could see that. Charlotte knew he couldn't control if she had coffee or not, but at the same time, she thought that he might already know what she wanted to talk about.

"Just a little cream and sugar," she said.

She didn't like her coffee overly sweet since she normally drank it with a baked good. Finn gently sat the cup down in front of her before he took a seat.

"What did you want to talk about?" he asked.

"You can go first," she whispered before she took a drink of her coffee.

Charlotte let out a sigh of content when the coffee tasted just how she liked it. He could make her coffee any time he wanted to, and she would be eternally grateful to him.

"No, mine can wait. Ladies first," he replied.

She took a deep breath in. How did she broach this? Did she just flat out tell him that she wanted him to be her Daddy, or did she say it subtly?

"I thought about what you said a couple of days ago," she said as she looked down at the coffee cup in her hands. "Last night just confirmed it for me. I want you to be my Daddy."

Charlotte didn't look up from her cup, worried that he wouldn't feel the same way now. What if last night he changed his mind and didn't want to be her Daddy any more? What if that's what he wanted to talk to her about today?

"Charlotte? Can you look at me?" he asked.

She slowly lifted her head and made eye contact with him. Dread filled her stomach as she waited for him to speak. Finn kept looking at her, searching her face for something, and Charlotte didn't know what.

"Charlotte," he said. "I would love to be your Daddy."

A grin spread across her face, and she couldn't help the giggle that escaped past her lips. Her heart was so happy that he felt the same way as her.

"Now, I had this contract pulled up because I was going to bring it up today. I know we've talked about this before, our red flags, what we like and don't like, willing to try, what our safe words are, my rules, and what you're comfortable with," Finn said as he pulled up his computer and turned it around. "How about you read this and tell me if anything looks wrong or if you want to add something."

Charlotte started to read the document and realized he was really paying attention when she talked about what she didn't like, liked, and all.

"We can always go back and add or change something if you want or I want later on," Finn added.

She nodded her head and finished up the last bit of the document. Everything looked good, and she was really surprised. Charlotte knew Daddy Doms were attentive, but they weren't in the serious phase at that point.

"Everything looks good," Charlotte said.

"Great! So you can type your name and put the date on there, and I'll do the same," Finn said.

She did as he said. Nerves and excitement danced in her stomach as she turned the computer around.

Her first Daddy and she couldn't wait. She couldn't wait to be taken care of, cherished, but also disciplined when needed.

"I want you to know that you can text or call me anytime for anything, and I'll pick up. I may not be able to pick up right away, but I'll call you as soon as I can. I do have meetings every once in a while, but I can normally pick up," Finn explained. "If you can't get a hold of me and need something right away, call Jaxson."

Charlotte nodded her head.

"I really mean it. You can't drive, scared of walking home in the dark." Finn thought for a second. "Actually, if you're walking home and it's dark or getting dark, you call me right away and wait for me to come get you. If you have an emergency, are scared, want snuggles, anything, please call me."

She nodded her head again. She understood that basically anything she needed to call him.

"Words, little one," he said.

"Yes, sir," she replied.

Finn raised an eyebrow, and Charlotte's cheeks turned bright red.

"Yes, Daddy," she said.

It felt so right for her to call him that, and she was glad she took ten seconds of courage and told him what she wanted.

"Good. If I find that you didn't call me and you got hurt, walked home in the dark, anything that put you in danger, or stuff like that, you will get a spanking." Finn's voice was level, and she knew he wasn't playing.

He was dead serious, and she needed to remember that. If his normal spankings were anything like the first night they met, Charlotte didn't want them. They hurt so bad, and she felt her bottom hours after when she rolled onto her back.

"Come here," Finn said, and he opened his arms.

Charlotte put her coffee cup down on the table and walked into his arms. He pulled her up to where she sat on his lap, a sigh of content escaping her mouth.

"I'm so glad you want to be my little one, my baby girl," he murmured on top of her head.

"Thank you," she whispered.

"For what, little one?"

"For being patient with me in the beginning."

"Anything for you."

Charlotte and Finn sat there in each other's embrace, both of them happy and content.

CHAPTER NINETEEN

CHARLOTTE

It had been several days since Charlotte had asked Finn to be her Daddy, and it was great. They were getting along, and she hadn't gotten in trouble yet, but Charlotte felt like she was going to get into trouble soon.

She had kept a secret from him, and she knew once he found out that it wasn't going to be good.

Finn had asked her several times if they could hang out, but Charlotte had to turn him down because she had work at the cafe. She came home every day and was exhausted. When Finn video called her every night, he could see, and she knew he had started to get worried.

He had asked several times if he could come over or if she could come to him, but she kept declining. Her pride had gotten in the way because she didn't want Finn to know that she had gotten a second job.

She didn't want to be a charity case for him, and she knew once she told him, he would tell her he could and would help her out. Charlotte didn't want to take all of his money because she couldn't be responsible enough with her own.

She was coming up on one of her days off, and she was going to tell her Daddy that she could finally hang out with him. She hoped he was available because she really wanted all the cuddles he could give her.

When Charlotte got home today from her shift at the cafe, she felt off. She hadn't been getting enough sleep the past several days, and she knew it was taking a toll on her body.

She was sluggish, cold but hot, and didn't want to eat anything. One of her coworkers had asked if she was okay, and Charlotte just brushed it off. She was tired, but it could just be from that.

She had been working more than she had been, and her body wasn't used to it. It was going to take her body a little while to get used to being worked this much before she got better.

She sat down on her couch and took several deep breaths. Her feet ached from being on them all day long. Her feet ached for the past several days nonstop, and she didn't know how to fix it. She tried to massage them, but it did nothing for them because once she stepped foot on them, they ached all over again.

Maybe she should ask her Daddy if he knew anything to help with feet that ached. He had to know something because he was a Daddy, and Daddies knew everything.

Just thinking about her Daddy made her want to call him. She was a needy little, and she didn't know if her Daddy liked that. He hadn't said anything, but at the same time, she hadn't called him or texted him as much as she would have.

Charlotte knew that he said to contact him with anything, but he was at work, and she also worked. She didn't want to bother him a lot with her neediness.

Her phone rang, and she quickly picked it up and saw that Daddy was calling.

"Hello?" She put her phone on speaker.

Charlotte felt like she was going to throw up, and she didn't want the phone in her hand when she had to make a run to the bathroom. She didn't have enough money to buy a new phone if she dropped and cracked it.

"Little one, you don't sound so good. Are you alright? Do I need to come over and take care of you?" he asked right off the bat.

Charlotte felt little when he talked to her like that. He cared, and it immediately made her little. She also didn't think she sounded that bad, but yet again she had heard her voice all day long and was biased.

"I is fine," she mumbled.

"Charlie." His voice went stern.

Charlotte shrunk into the couch. She didn't like it when he used his stern voice at her. It made her feel extremely small, and he wasn't with her right now to look after her.

"Can I talk to big Charlotte?" Finn asked.

She let out a sigh and took several deep breaths. She needed to get her mind in the right spot to talk to him as an adult and not her little side.

"Yes?" she whispered. She didn't feel confident at all that she wouldn't fall into little space again.

"Are you feeling alright? What's wrong?" he asked.

"I'm okay, just tired," she said honestly.

Charlotte didn't want to lie to him anymore. She was tired, and they both knew it.

"How much sleep have you been getting?" Finn asked.

She thought about it for a second. She had gotten eight hours of sleep the night before, but before that it was only six hours.

"Last night I got eight hours," she said.

"And the night before?"

Charlotte let out a sigh. She knew her Daddy wanted her to get at least eight hours of sleep each night, but it was hard when she worked another job. She had to get home and eat something small before she could take a shower and go to bed.

"Charlotte, don't lie to me," Daddy said.

"Six hours," she softly said.

She knew he heard her when he let out a sigh.

"For how many nights?" he asked.

She knew that was coming next. She was in trouble, and she couldn't do anything about it. Charlotte hadn't followed what her Daddy wanted her to do, and she had to pay for it.

"Four or five nights. I can't remember." She sat up straight on the couch.

She felt worse now, and it was only growing. Charlotte didn't know if it was only because she had lied to him about her sleep or if it was because she had kept this secret for a while.

Daddy had asked her why she was so busy the other day, and she lied. She said she had a project going on at home and he couldn't see it. A big fat lie, and she knew when he found out it wasn't going to be good. She just didn't want to tell him that she had a second job.

"You know the rules," he said over the phone. She heard the disappointment in his voice, and she felt even worse about it now. "What is the rule?"

"To get at least eight hours of sleep," she replied.

"That's right, little one. Do you know why?"

She nodded her head but quickly started to speak because he couldn't see her. "To keep me healthy."

"That's right. I want you to be healthy, and getting less than eight hours of sleep can make you feel bad and be in a bad mood," he said. "I don't want that."

"I know." She let out a sigh.

She hated that she disappointed her Daddy. Charlotte knew now that he couldn't find out about her financial position or that she worked a second job. She didn't want to see or hear the disappointment.

"I really want to see you right now, but I know you need to get into bed. Do you work tomorrow?" he asked.

"I don't work tomorrow," she replied.

She knew her punishment was going to be tomorrow. Charlotte just had a feeling.

"Can we hang out tomorrow? I don't have any meetings," he said.

"Okay."

She didn't know what else to say. She wanted to hang out with her Daddy, but she didn't want to get her punishment.

"You know you're getting a punishment tomorrow. You broke a rule, and it can't go unpunished," he said.

"I know." Charlotte's voice was so small.

"It's going to be okay. After the punishment, all is forgiven," Daddy said.

Not all would be forgiven because he didn't know about

the other things she had kept from him. He didn't know, and she was going to feel guilty until he found out or until he wasn't her Daddy anymore.

Charlotte didn't know if she could feel guilty the whole time he was her Daddy, and she didn't want him to not be her Daddy. She loved it, and she couldn't see herself with anyone else.

"Okay, well, you need to go to bed," Daddy said.

She didn't want to hang up and not talk to him anymore.

"I'll be at your house at nine in the morning," he said. "Don't eat breakfast 'cause I'll make you some."

"Okay, thank you," she replied.

"Good night, little one."

"Good night, Daddy." Her voice sounded so sad.

Neither of them hung up.

"Do you want me to come over, little one?" he asked. "You sound sad."

"I'm okay. Just tired. I'm going to take a bath and then go to bed."

Daddy took a breath in. "No bath. I don't want you to slip in the tub when I'm not around. Take a quick shower, and then go to bed."

"Okay, Daddy."

She could see where he was coming from. One time Charlotte had overheard a conversation at BTS. The Daddy had said his little one had taken a bath while he was right next to her, and she slipped. The little froze and didn't come up for air but stayed under water.

Charlotte didn't want that, and it scared her. Any time she had taken a bath by herself, the water was so low that if she had slipped, her face would still be above water.

It wasn't fun to play in water that was so shallow, but she didn't want to drown.

"Good night, little one. I'll see you in the morning," Daddy said. "Don't forget to plug your phone in before you go to bed."

"Good night, Daddy," she replied.

Daddy hung up the phone, and Charlotte let out a sigh. She didn't want to get up, but she knew she needed to go take a shower and get into bed. She didn't want to add on to her punishment even more by not getting eight hours of sleep.

Charlotte got up from the couch and made her way toward the bathroom. She had placed clothes in here before she left for work because she knew once she got home she wasn't going to want to.

"Maybe I can just skip my shower," she whispered to herself. "No, no. I smell so bad. Baked goods and coffee. I don't want my bed smelling like that."

With her mind made up, she turned on the shower to the right temperature before she stepped in. She washed her hair first before she moved to her body. As she rinsed off the soap, the water turned off.

"That's odd," she mumbled.

Charlotte tried to turn the water off and on before it clicked in her brain.

"Shit," she whispered. "This can't be happening."

They had turned the water off. Charlotte didn't think the two weeks had passed, but when she remembered what today was, she realized it had.

Charlotte grabbed her towel and wrapped it around herself. She had to think for a second. She didn't know how much more money she had to go before she could pay the water bill.

Maybe she could shower at the club or the bakery when no one was there. She had seen Amelia do it when she got really messy at the bakery. Charlotte could spill something on herself and take a shower.

She knew that she needed to figure something out because she would smell after a couple shifts at the bakery and cafe. There was no way around it. She sweated too much after she worked at both places.

Right as Charlotte stepped out of the bathroom, her lights started to flicker.

"No, no, no." Her voice raised as she talked.

The electricity couldn't be going off at the same time. She wouldn't be able to handle that as well. Charlotte didn't like the dark.

The lights turned off, and Charlotte let out a scream. She scampered to her bed and got under the covers.

"I can do this. Just fall asleep," Charlotte whispered to herself.

Her whole body shook as she laid in her bed. She took several deep breaths in to try and calm herself down. She just needed to fall asleep, but Charlotte knew she wouldn't be able to.

How long would it take for her to pass out from exhaustion? Charlotte didn't know, but she hoped it would be soon.

CHAPTER TWENTY

CHARLOTTE

*C*harlotte slowly woke up from slumber, and it took her a couple minutes to realize where she was. She felt a lot worse than she had before she fell back asleep, and she didn't know why.

Could she be getting sick? She hadn't gotten sick in years, and she didn't want to get sick now. She had to work two jobs so she could pay for her electric and water bill.

She needed those to be paid for so she could relax some. That's all Charlotte wanted to do right now.

She opened her eyes and realized she was still under her covers, shaking from how cold it was in the room. She knew she hadn't been asleep long because her hair was still damp from the shower. Which meant it was still dark outside.

A shiver ran through Charlotte at the thought of it being dark. With the electricity cut off, she didn't have her night-light anymore.

The floorboards creaked, and Charlotte let out a little scream. Was someone in the house? Should she call Diana or her Daddy about this? Wait for them to come and see if anyone was in her house.

She didn't want to call either of them since it was late at night, but she knew she had to. If either of them found out that her water and electricity turned off and she didn't call either one of them, it wouldn't be good.

Daddy would know when he came tomorrow to pick her up. What if he asked to use the bathroom and couldn't flush or wash his hands? She needed to call him or Diana.

"H-hello?" she timidly called out.

She didn't know what else to do in this situation besides call out or look. Right now, she wasn't brave enough to look out from under the covers.

There wasn't any noise after she called out which made her relax a little. Maybe she could look out since there wasn't any noise.

Charlotte took a deep breath in before she peaked from under the cover. Her eyes immediately went to the corner, and she let out a scream before she realized it was just clothes hanging up on a couch.

With her mind made up, she scampered across her bed and grabbed her phone. Her towel was long gone on her bed, and she started to shiver from the cold air hitting her bare skin. She really needed to get clothes on, but she also needed to call her Daddy. Charlotte didn't want to wait any longer in this house alone.

She turned her phone on to realize it was at five percent battery. Charlotte had forgotten to plug it in before the water and electricity turned off. Her mind was too scared, and she forgot Daddy's reminder to plug it in.

Charlotte dialed Daddy's number and put it against her

ear. She hoped that Daddy would pick up before her phone died.

"Hello?" His husky voice filtered through the phone. "Charlotte? What's wrong?"

"I d-don't feel good, and I'm s-scared," Charlotte managed to get out through her chattering teeth. "Can you come get me?"

She waited for his response, but none came. Did he not want to come pick her up in the middle of the night? He had said she could call him at any point, and he would help. Did he lie?

Charlotte brought the phone away from her head and realized it had died. Dread filled her stomach. Did Daddy catch any of what Charlotte had said, or did he miss all of it? She hoped he got her message.

She got off the bed and quickly made her way to her closet to grab Daddy's shirt and sweatpants and put them on. Charlotte didn't want to be inside this house for one more second. It was creepy at night, and her imagination was going to run wild if she heard any more noise.

Charlotte ran out of her house and sat on the steps as she waited for her Daddy to come. She didn't like to be outside alone, but there were street lights, so Charlotte could see more than in her house.

She had no clue if he was actually coming, but she hoped he was. Charlotte didn't know what else she was going to do if her Daddy didn't come to get her. She didn't have any phone battery to call Diana, and she knew her neighbors wouldn't answer.

They had never answered and weren't friendly. All Charlotte wanted to do was curl up under covers and be warm.

She was shivering at this point; her nose was stuffy and her body ached as she sat on the steps waiting for her Daddy to come get her.

She leaned her head against the railing and took several deep breaths in. Charlotte knew she needed to stay calm until Daddy came to get her, but it was harder than it seemed.

Her body was shivering the longer she was outside. She didn't know how long she was going to be able to stay outside for. What if Daddy never came for her? What if he just thought it was a butt dial and he went back to bed?

Charlotte closed her eyes as she felt the achiness and weight of everything come down on her. She was so tired, and she was worried she would fall asleep before Daddy got here.

The wind blew past her, and Charlotte pulled her legs up to her chest. She should've grabbed a jacket when she got dressed, but it wasn't a priority for her at the time. Her priority was to call her Daddy, get dressed, and get out of the house.

Charlotte wanted to go back in and grab a jacket, but she didn't want to go back into the dark scary house. Not until it was light or someone else was with her.

She blinked several times when she heard a car stop in front of her house. Charlotte couldn't make out who was in it. Fear rolled through her as the person got out.

Who could it be?

CHAPTER TWENTY-ONE

FINN

Finn woke up abruptly to Charlotte when she called him. He didn't know what Charlotte would want at three in the morning, but it didn't matter. He told her when they first got together that she could call at any time for anything, and he meant it.

Charlotte didn't give Finn much before she ended the call. So many thoughts ran through his head as he drove to her house. Why did she end the call? Why did he need him to come?

She said she didn't feel well, and he could hear it in her voice. He had no doubt that she was sick. Finn had asked her before she went to take a shower because she didn't sound good, but she just said it was because she was tired.

He should've pushed harder to get her to agree for him to come over. He knew she was starting to get sick, and he wanted to help and should have. Finn should've told her he was coming over or she was coming to his house, but either way, he should have insisted they be together.

Finn had quickly put on a shirt and sweats before he ran

outside to his car. He wanted to get there as soon as possible, and he was thankful that he had saved her address in his phone when he dropped her off.

He pulled up to her driveway and saw a figure sitting on the porch steps. Had she been sitting outside since the call? Why was she outside in this weather?

Finn got out of the car and made his way to her.

"Charlotte?" he called out, trying to gain her attention.

Her eyes were open, and she looked at him, but it felt off. How long had she been sitting out for?

"Daddy?" Her voice was hoarse, and she started to cough.

She was definitely getting sick, and he needed to get her out of this cold weather. What was she thinking when she sat out here in only his shirt and sweats?

He knew she hadn't been thinking because she wasn't feeling good, and he couldn't blame her for that right now. Finn needed to get her inside and quickly.

"Little one, how long have you been out here?" he softly asked as he knelt in front of her.

He had asked a couple of times to go inside her house or take care of her in there, but she always turned him down. Finn didn't know if she was embarrassed because it was messy or if she was hiding something. He didn't want to just barge into her house with her in his arms and break her trust when she got better.

Finn jogged back to his car and got his extra hoodie from the back. He always had a hoodie in his car in case of emergencies, and right now, he was grateful for that.

He helped get it on Charlotte, so she wasn't as cold while he tried to get her to allow him to go into her house.

"Charlotte, can you tell me how long you've been out here for?" he asked again.

She shrugged her shoulders. Finn wondered if she even knew how long she'd been out here for.

"Did you come out after you called me?" he asked.

She nodded her head, and Finn cursed under his breath. She had been out here for over fifteen minutes in nothing but his sweats and shirt.

From her voice on the call, he knew she was getting sick, and this no doubt made it worse. Finn didn't like that she was getting sick, but he also couldn't help but feel a little joyed by it. She would be needy, most littles were, and he couldn't wait.

Finn had wanted her to rely on him more, but he could understand that it had only been over a week since they formally agreed for him to be her Daddy. She was still getting used to it, and he didn't want to rush her into anything and make her regret it.

"Come on, let's get you inside." Finn went to pick her up.

Charlotte whimpered and shook her head. He let out a sigh but nodded his head.

"Can you tell me what's wrong? Why did you call me?" he asked.

She leaned her head against the railing again and closed her eyes.

"No, don't close your eyes. I need you to stay awake for me." Finn picked her up.

She whined but stilled in his arms as he started to rock back and forth. He knew she didn't feel well, but he needed to know why she called him. He didn't know what was wrong besides the fact that she didn't feel good. Was that all, or was there something else?

"Charlotte, I need you to tell me," Finn said, his voice not asking but telling her.

She buried her head into his shoulder, and Finn started to worry.

"Charlotte."

"It's nothing. I just don't feel good," she mumbled against his chest.

Finn knew she was lying, and he was going to figure out the truth.

"It's not nothing. There's something else you aren't telling me," Finn said.

Charlotte started to shake in his hold, and for a second, he thought she was cold, but then he heard the sniffles. She was crying.

"Oh, little one, what's wrong?" he asked. "You can tell Daddy anything."

She shook her head and continued to cry in his arms. He hated not knowing what was bothering her. Finn wanted to make everything alright. He didn't want her to be sad, and yet she was.

"Little cupcake, tell Daddy what's wrong." He gently rubbed her back. "Daddy needs to know so he can make it better."

Charlotte continued to sniffle but pulled away from him.

"I lied," she wailed in his arms.

He stared at her in shock. What could she have lied to him about? Finn wracked his brain to try and figure out what she could be talking about.

"What did you lie about?" His voice was calm.

He didn't want to spook her, so he tried to keep his voice calm. She was sick, didn't feel well, probably scared, and he didn't want to add on to it.

"I've lied about doing a project at my house! I've been working a second job to get money to pay for my electric and water bill." She whimpered at the end.

Finn kept his face neutral, so he didn't spook Charlotte, but he was shocked. He had no clue that she was hurting for money right now. That she had been trying to pay her bill and had to get a second job.

How could he have let this slip through his fingers?

Finn knew something had been up in the past week, but he couldn't tell what. He tried to probe and get an answer, but she wouldn't give any besides having a project in her house she was working on.

"I'm sorry, little cupcake. You should've told Daddy so he could help out," Finn said. "I would've helped in any way you needed me to."

Charlotte shook her head. "No charity case," she mumbled.

Finn had a feeling that she was stubborn and wouldn't take any money she didn't work hard for. He was proud, but he also wished she would accept more help from people.

"Did something happen tonight besides you feeling icky?" Finn asked.

She nodded her head, and tears fell down her face again.

"Can you tell Daddy?"

Finn could see the hesitance in her posture and facial expression.

"Please? Daddy wants to make it all better," he said and laid a kiss on her forehead.

Finn frowned. Her forehead felt hot, and he knew it wasn't good. She had been outside for a long time, and she shouldn't be this warm. When they get to his house, he'll definitely be checking her temperature.

"My water and electricity got turned off." She looked at his chest.

His heart broke a little at her words. He couldn't believe that he didn't pry more when he felt off about things. He wasn't being a very good Daddy, and that was going to change.

Finn had wanted to give her space, but now he knew she didn't need as much as he gave her. She needed more rules, and he needed to ask a lot of questions.

"When did that happen, little cupcake?" he asked.

"Soon after we said goodbye last night," she whispered.

Finn took a breath in. She was safe now, and he was going to take care of her when they got to his house.

"Here's what we're going to do," Finn said. "Can you pay attention to Daddy right now?"

Charlotte looked up at him, tears in her eyes.

"We're going to go inside your house and pack you clothes and anything you might need for the next couple of days. You'll be staying at Daddy's house while you recover," he explained as he took a step up the stairs.

She shook her head feverishly and let out a whimper. He watched as Charlotte grabbed her head and closed her eyes tightly.

"It's not up for discussion. We're doing this so you're safe. You're sick, and I can't have you being alone. I haven't been a good Daddy the past week, and that's changing," he said.

"No," she whimpered. "No go back in."

Finn held her close to his body and rocked her slightly. He wanted her to calm down because she was starting to work herself into a fit, and he wasn't going to have that.

"Do you want to sit in Daddy's car while he goes in and gets your stuff?" Finn asked.

He didn't know why Charlotte was starting to throw a fit, but he was determined to figure it out. Charlotte shook her head and clung onto his neck.

"Then why do you not want to go in?"

Charlotte put her head on his shoulder. "It's messy."

"I've told you before that I don't care if your house is messy," Finn replied. He had told her several times that he didn't mind.

His house was clean because that's how he liked it, but some people didn't like clean houses.

"Why else do you not want to go in there?" he asked.

It couldn't be just because the house was messy. Deep inside, he knew it wasn't that and that there was something else.

"I'm embarrassed to say," she mumbled.

What could she be embarrassed about?

Finn thought back to everything that happened. The electricity was out. Charlotte was outside when he got here and not inside.

His eyes went wide.

"Little cupcake, are you afraid of the dark?" he asked.

It all started to make sense now. Her house was probably pitch dark in there, and she was scared. Outside there are a couple street lights that she would be able to see around her.

Charlotte nodded her head against his shoulder, and he relaxed a little bit. He could work with her being scared of the dark. It just meant he could protect her from the monsters in the closets and under the bed.

"Charlotte, can you look at Daddy?" Finn asked.

Her head came out of his shoulder, and she looked at him. He could see her glassy eyes from being sick but also from tears in her eyes.

"You don't need to be afraid when Daddy's here. Daddy will protect you from the monsters and the dark." He ran his hand up and down her back as he tried to calm her down. "When we go in, you'll be in my arms the whole time or holding my hand, so the monsters can't get you."

Charlotte's eyes started to fill with tears, and it broke his heart that she was so afraid of the dark. What could have happened to make her this scared?

"Does that sound like a good plan?" Finn asked. "You'll be safe with Daddy."

Charlotte nodded her head. "Okay, Daddy."

His heart warmed that she trusted him so much with protecting her from the monsters. Now he just needed to get her to trust him for every other aspect of their lives.

It wasn't going to be easy, but Finn was up for the challenge.

CHAPTER TWENTY-TWO

CHARLOTTE

harlotte felt overwhelmed with everything that had been going on. She hadn't felt well, and Daddy was asking her a lot of questions. All she wanted to do was sleep and be warm. Preferably in his arms but Charlotte wasn't going to verbalize that right now.

When Daddy had put his hoodie on her, she wanted to cry. She was so cold, and he had thought about her. And the way he held her as she cried in his arms. She felt so cherished and loved at that moment, which made her cry even harder.

But it all got ruined when he asked to go into her house to grab some of her things. She didn't want him to go into her house, and she didn't want him to find out that she didn't have electricity or water, but that didn't happen.

Her Daddy had asked, and she knew she was already in trouble because she kept this a secret but also because she had disobeyed several rules already. She was in a lot of trouble already, and she was only adding on to the punishment. Charlotte didn't want to lie to her Daddy anymore because she already felt guilty.

The tight knot of guilt had been weighing down in her stomach for over a week. It made her nauseous every time she thought about it, which was constant. Charlotte couldn't get it out of her mind, and it was slowly starting to drive her crazy.

She knew she had to tell her Daddy soon, and it did come, but the guilt was still there. Charlotte didn't know why it was still there since she had told Daddy about it. The guilt should've been gone, but it wasn't.

"Little cupcake?" Daddy called out.

Charlotte loved it every time he called her that; she also liked when he called her little one, but little cupcake had a special meaning. Daddy knew she loved cupcakes, and the name stuck. It brought her joy every time he called her that, even when she felt icky.

No one had ever called her little one or little cupcake before, and it made her feel special. So special that she wanted to be called that all the time now.

She was trying to stall as long as she could so they didn't have to go into her house. It was a mess, but she also had never had a male in her house before. Charlotte had no doubt he wouldn't do anything bad, but she was worried he wouldn't like it.

She wanted her Daddy to love her as she was, but she was worried she might be too much. Too messy and irresponsible. Her Daddy didn't even know that she was hurting for money, but she figured he knew by her water and electricity being turned off.

Charlotte put her hands on each side of her head. Everything was getting to be too much for her, and she was getting overwhelmed.

Would he understand that she'd never had a man inside her house? Would he think it was weird?

Tears of frustration rolled down her face. She wanted her brain to turn off so she didn't have to think about any of this anymore.

"What's wrong?" Daddy asked as he pulled Charlotte once again out of her thoughts. "You can tell Daddy what's wrong."

"I-I d-don't want you to go inside because no man has ever been in there before." She got less confident as she talked, her voice going quieter as time went on. "I w-want my brain to turn off. So many thoughts."

She was embarrassed to admit that. Charlotte had heard several girls talking about how they had guys come over all the time, and she wasn't like that. Charlotte wasn't a virgin, but since she had moved into this house, she hadn't had anyone over really. She didn't have a lot of friends, but maybe Janie could come over soon.

She had gotten really comfortable around Janie, and she believed they were friends now. They could have a playdate in her little room. Well, once the electricity and water bill got paid for. She needed to do that first before she had her over.

"Charlotte," her Daddy said.

She looked down at his chest. She kept zoning out, and she couldn't help it.

"Sowwy," she whispered.

Charlotte wanted to be little right now. When she felt icky and tired, she just wanted to be little so she didn't have to think about much. She wanted to give her worries to her Daddy so he could just take care of her, but right now, she wasn't doing that.

She was still trying to control everything because she was embarrassed.

"I need you to pay attention to Daddy." He brought her face up to look at him. "Does Daddy have your attention?"

Charlotte nodded her head.

"Good girl. I promise I won't look much. All I want to do is get you some clothes, stuffies, toiletries, and anything else you might need for the next couple of days," he said.

She nodded her head again. It sounded like heaven to go to his house and be taken care of, but would she give up all the control for her Daddy to do that?

"Is that okay with you if Daddy goes in to grab some clothes and other things you might need?" he asked.

"Y-you'll be with me the w-whole time?" she stuttered, fear coursing through her body with the thought of going in and being separated from him.

Did he have a night-light at his house?

"Wait!" she screeched and then went into a coughing fit.

Her throat was dry, and she didn't feel good at all. Charlotte felt like she could throw up at any moment, and she really hoped she didn't. She hated to throw up.

Daddy's eyes went wide as he stared at her. "What is it, little cupcake? What has you worked up?"

Charlotte leaned in closer to him, right next to his ear. "D-do you have a night-light?"

She leaned back and looked at her Daddy's face. What if he didn't have one? Would she be able to take hers with her to use?

Daddy beckoned her closer with his empty hand, and she leaned forward.

"I have two night-lights," he whispered in her ear. "Is that enough, or do I need to go buy more?"

She shook her head. "That's enough."

"Good. Now, I promise you I'll be with you the whole time. You'll either be in my arms, or you'll be holding my hand, but I'll always be with you."

Charlotte let out a sigh of relief and placed her head on his shoulder.

"Otay, I'm weady, I guess," she mumbled.

She felt Daddy start to walk into her house, and she covered her face with her hands. She didn't want to see his reaction to her messy living room or her house in general.

"Can you tell Daddy where your bedroom is?" he asked.

Charlotte pointed to the back corner of the house where there was a hallway. That's where her room and her little room was.

"Right side," she said before relaxing in his hold again.

Daddy started to walk in that direction, and right as he started to open the door, Charlotte realized she said the wrong room.

"Wait," she weakly said, but it was too late.

Charlotte stared at her Daddy with wide eyes. She knew he had to know that she had a room like this, but she didn't want him to see it just yet. It was the messiest room of them all, and she wasn't proud of it.

She didn't have any rules about cleaning up after herself, and so she didn't. Charlotte didn't have a reason to clean up after herself because she'd end up using it again. She didn't know what the point of cleaning up after herself in her play-room was for.

"Is this my little cupcake's playroom?" daddy asked.

Charlotte looked around, and she nodded her head.

"My little cupcake is so messy," he baby talked to her. "So messy but that's okay. Daddy will help make sure his little cupcake cleans up after herself."

Charlotte was mortified. It wasn't her fault, it was her stuffies' fault. They knew that they shouldn't have distracted her, but they did it anyway.

"Other room," Charlotte whispered.

How could she have forgotten that her room was on the left side and not the right? That wasn't like her, but she couldn't be too hard on herself right now. She wasn't feeling good, and her brain was all foggy.

She couldn't think straight, and it annoyed her. She should've been able to remember which side her room was in and which side her playroom was in.

"It's okay, little cupcake," Daddy whispered in her ear. "You're okay. I promise I'll forget everything I saw, and when you're ready to show me this room, I'll see it for the first time."

Charlotte knew that it didn't work that way, but she couldn't help but relax. She knew deep down he wouldn't forget, but it didn't matter. He promised that he would, and she believed him.

"Now, do you need anything else besides clothes and toiletries? Do you have a bag that we can put anything in?"

Charlotte pointed to her closet where everything was.

"Just stuff things in," she mumbled. She didn't want to be here any longer.

"Can you say that again? Do you need a stuffie?" Daddy asked.

Her head perked up at the mention of her stuffie. She had

several stuffies, but she had a favorite one, and it laid on her bed.

"Moody!" Her voice raised, and she wiggled in her Daddy's arms.

"Who's Moody, little cupcake?" Daddy asked.

Charlotte pointed to the big blue hippo on her bed. Daddy turned around and let out a gasp.

"Such a pretty stuffie," he said as he walked toward her bed and picked up Moody.

Satisfied, Charlotte held Moody close to her as her Daddy walked back to the closet with her still in his arms. She felt safe and secure in his arms as he packed her bags.

"My little cupcake, can you stay awake for a couple more minutes?" Finn asked. "Then you can go to sleep when we get into the car."

Charlotte nodded and took her head off of his shoulder.

"Do you have anything for your little that you want before we leave your house?" he asked.

She thought about it for a second but couldn't think of anything.

"I d-don't know," she whispered.

Daddy rubbed her back. "It's okay. If you forget anything, we can come back and grab it."

Charlotte nodded her head and relaxed in his embrace.

"Okay," he whispered. "We're going to have a sleepover at my house for a couple of days. We're going to get you all better. We don't want you feeling icky any more, and I'm going to take care of you and make you all better."

Snuggled in his embrace, Charlotte relaxed fully as he walked out of the house with her bag of things. Her hold on

Moody was tight as they walked through the dark because she was scared and her eyes were closed.

"It's okay," Daddy softly spoke to her. "You're okay. We're almost out of the house. Daddy's got you."

The breeze brushed against her skin as they stepped outside.

"We're outside now. You can open your eyes," he said.

Charlotte didn't open her eyes though. The exhaustion had seeped into her body as she relaxed into her Daddy's embrace.

"Tired," she mumbled as her head rested on his shoulder.

He gently placed her into his car seat and buckled her in.

"Daddy's going to need to get you a booster seat," he said and kissed her on her forehead.

"Nooo," she whined.

Finn chuckled but didn't say anything. "You can sleep now. I'll carry you into my house."

Snuggled into the car seat, Charlotte held Moody close to her and fell asleep.

CHAPTER TWENTY-THREE

FINN

Finn didn't know what to think as he drove them back to his house. There were so many alarms that went off in his head as he walked through her house and talked to her more.

He knew she was definitely sick. Charlotte had kept zoning in an out, not understanding, scratchy voice, hot and shivering, and not moving fast at all. He had her in his arms the whole time, but when she moved her head to his shoulder and off his shoulder, it was slow like she was in pain.

How had she gotten sick? Why was she so exhausted? Why did her electric and water get turned off? Why did she stay outside and wait for him?

So many thoughts ran through his head that he started to feel a headache form. The pressure built up, and he knew when he got home that he was going to have to take medicine. But first he needed to make sure that Charlotte was okay.

She always came first.

He didn't like that she waited this long to call him. It had

186

been hours since they had gotten off the phone, and that's when the water and electricity turned off.

Hours of her being in the dark when she was afraid. Hours of her getting sicker and not being taken care of.

Finn wanted to beat himself up for it. Maybe he could have Marco spar with him soon, and Marco could beat the shit out of him. He needed it because he had done a bad job of taking care of Charlotte. He let so many things slip because he didn't want to overwhelm her and scare her off, but he knew he made a mistake.

He should've gone with his gut and pushed a little harder, gotten her to allow her to come over before she fell asleep so he could take care of her.

Finn knew for next time. Well, there wasn't going to be a next time if he could help it. Charlotte wasn't going to go through this again, and he promised himself that.

She deserved the world on a golden platter. Anything she wanted, he was going to try and get for her. Finn had a feeling that she wasn't going to ask for anything, which meant he would have to get the information out of her.

Easy for him. He knew how to ask questions and get an answer out of her. She liked it when he commanded that she tell him, her body language and facial expression told him that.

Finn knew that in certain situations she wasn't going to tell him things because she wasn't comfortable. That was okay, for a certain amount of time. He didn't want to force her to tell him anything, but he also didn't want her to get away with anything or not come to him because she was embarrassed.

There was nothing to be embarrassed about between a

Daddy and his little girl. In Finn's case, a Daddy and his little cupcake.

Oh, he knew she loved it when he called her that. The way the little shiver went through her body as he called her that. Or the small smile that would appear on her face.

Finn didn't know if she was aware that she did that, and he wasn't going to tell her yet. He didn't want to tell her and then she stop doing it because she was self conscious. Not going to happen on his watch because he loved the little smile and shiver that went through her when he called her that.

He couldn't wait to see what else she liked to be called. His good little girl? He bet that one would make her feel all gooey inside, and he couldn't wait to call her that.

Finn briefly looked over at Charlotte and couldn't help but worry about her. Why didn't she come to him sooner about this? Did she not feel comfortable? Did he make her feel like she couldn't come to him for anything?

He didn't like the thought of that, and it worried him. When they first talked about being in a dynamic together, he had told her that she could come to him for anything. Charlotte had said she understood, but that didn't mean she was going to. He needed to let her know that she could come to him for anything and that he wanted her to.

Maybe she didn't think it was that important? Or that she didn't want to bother him?

Finn didn't know, but he was going to find out when she got better. With that thought, he knew he needed to call Michael.

Michael was one of the eight owners of BTS, and before they decided to open the club, he was a doctor. He still practiced some but not as much as he used to. Finn knew that when they got to his house he would call him right away; he didn't care that it was four almost five in the morning.

He needed to make sure that Charlotte was going to be okay and what exactly to do. Finn didn't know if she just had a cold or if it was something else, but he was going to find out.

With a sigh, Finn pulled into his parking garage for his house. Should he put her in the nursery he had or in his bed? He wanted her to be comfortable, but he also didn't want to freak her out if she was in his bed.

The crib could possibly make her feel secure if she woke up in the middle of the night. He would just have to make sure to put a nightlight in before he left, in case she did wake up. Finn didn't want Charlotte to wake up and be scared.

With that in mind, Finn got out of the car and walked around to Charlotte. He loved having her in his arms, and he couldn't wait until she woke up. Maybe she would be all snuggly while she was feeling icky and want to be held. Finn didn't care if he got sick, all he wanted was to give Charlotte all the love and affection she wanted and needed.

He carried her into his house and up to the second floor where the nursery was. Finn had never brought a little girl to his nursery. It never felt right until now.

He had wanted to bring Charlotte to his nursery the first time he met her, which shocked him. He wasn't like that, and he knew it.

Maybe once she saw it she would want to move in. Finn wouldn't object to that because he wanted her to move in.

If he had it his way, she would've been moved in already, but it wasn't up to him, and he knew that. But Finn did know that if she was lying about not wanting to move in or scared, he would ease those worries and give her a little push, a little nudge in the right direction.

He would try his best not to be biased, but he knew it would be hard.

The crib came into view, and Finn found himself not wanting to put her down. He wanted to continue to hold her in his arms.

But Finn knew that he needed to call Michael to ask him to come and check on Charlotte. Finn wouldn't stop worrying until he came.

He gently placed Charlotte down in the crib and made sure the bar was locked in place. He didn't want her waking up and trying to climb out only for it to not be in place and her fault. He didn't want her climbing over anyways, but he didn't know what she was gonna do when she woke up if he wasn't there.

Fin grabbed his phone and called Michael.

"It's five in the morning," Michael answered.

"You know I wouldn't call you this early if I didn't have a good reason," Finn replied.

Finn has only called Michael a handful of times. He didn't like bothering people, but he'd never really needed to call Michael outside of work. They hung out some, but they both are busy.

"I know. What do you need?"

Finn let out a sigh. "Could you come over and examine someone?"

"Does this someone have a name?"

"She does. Her name is Charlotte, and she's my little one if you haven't heard already."

Finn had no doubt that the other owners knew he had

found someone, his little girl. He wasn't mad, but people talked, and he knew it.

"The cute little you were with the other night?" Michael asked.

"That's her."

"What's wrong?"

"She may be getting a cold, but I'm not quite sure. She sounded off when I called her last night around ten, and then I picked her up at three-thirty, and she sounded and looked worse."

"A sick little. That's not fun. I'll be there in five minutes."

Michael hung up, and Finn sat an on the couch in the kitchen. He hoped that she wouldn't be too sick, that it was just a minor cold that would go away in a couple days.

A knock sounded on the door, and Finn got up to go answer it.

"When did you first notice her getting sick?" Michael asked coming in, not waiting for pleasantries.

It was like Michael to just go straight into business, and Finn liked that.

"I knew she was getting tired and not enough sleep whenever we called each night. It wasn't until tonight that I realized she was starting to get sick."

Finn regretted not keeping a closer eye on her. He should've been more diligent in making sure that she got at least eight hours of sleep each night and eat healthy.

"She works at the bakery?"

He wasn't surprised that Michael already knew this. Michael, Jaxson, or someone else probably told him that she worked there.

"Yes, she works there in the morning. I don't know. She has a second job now."

Finn hated that he knew she got a second job because it meant she was overworking herself. She already didn't get enough sleep when she just worked at the bakery, but to add in a second job would make it worse.

"What do you mean?"

"She called me at three in a panic and didn't sound good. When I got there, she was outside, wearing a shirt and sweatpants, freezing cold. After a while, I got the information out, and she told me that her electricity and water got turned off," Finn explained. "Thinking back to the last week, she was not wanting to hang out in the afternoons and said she had a project going on, but it makes sense that she got a second job."

"And you didn't know that?"

Finn shook his head. "I didn't, and I really wish I did, but that's in the past now, and all I can do is make it better in the future. Make it better now."

"Good."

Before any of them could say anything more, they heard a little scream.

"Daddy!" Charlotte yelled.

Her voice was scratchy and hoarse, like she was about to lose it. Finn grimaced and started walking toward her.

It didn't take long for them to walk into the nursery. Charlotte was lying on her back.

"Hello, my little cupcake," Finn said as he lowered the railing on the side.

Charlotte had tears in her eyes, and Finn quickly picked her up and held her close.

"Shhh. It's okay," Finn whispered in her ear. "Everything's gonna be okay. You're safe."

She buried her face in Finn's neck and relaxed a little.

"I'm gonna want to take her temperature first, see if she's running a fever, and then I'll do other assessments," Michael said, breaking the silence.

Charlotte flinched and held onto Finn tighter.

"It's okay, little cupcake. This is one of Daddy's friends. His name is Michael, and he used to be a doctor," Finn explained.

"No need doctor. I'm fine," she mumbled.

He chuckled and slowly rocked Charlotte in his arms.

"I bet you're feeling a little icky. Daddy called his friend to make you get all better."

Charlotte wiggled in his arms, but he held her securely to him. But Charlotte didn't stop moving. With a quick movement, Finn swatted her bottom, and she stilled.

"Charlotte's going to be a good girl while Michael checks her over."

"No doctor!"

Finn placed Charlotte on the changing table and effortlessly strapped her down, so she wasn't able to move. He didn't want her to hurt herself.

"Can you either turn her on her side or pull her legs up like you would put a diaper on her?" Michael asked.

Knowing what he wanted, Finn pulled her sweats down and realized she didn't have any underwear on. That made it easier for Michael to be able to insert the thermometer.

"Daddy! Nooo!" Charlotte wailed.

"Hush," he replied. "Be a good girl for Daddy, and let Michael check your temperature."

Charlotte pulled her hands up to her face and covered it. Finn had no doubt she was embarrassed, but she shouldn't be. This would become a regular thing to ensure she stayed healthy.

After this, Finn might check her temperature every morning to make sure she didn't get sick again.

"Would it be wise to check her temperature every morning?" Finn asked as Michael pulled out everything he needed from his bag.

Finn was relieved that he was able to come and that he knew Michael. If Michael wasn't able to come, he would have taken Charlotte to the emergency room. He didn't want to take any chances of her being sick and not getting better.

"For the next couple of days, I would, just to make sure her fever is still there or going away," Michael said. "But after is up to you. If you want to check every morning, I don't think it would be a bad idea. If you don't, then I would check it maybe once a week."

Finn nodded his head and looked back at Charlotte. Her eyes were closed under her fingers, and he knew the next couple of minutes would be hard for her.

"Ready?" Michael asked Finn.

He held her legs up higher in the air and watched as Michael lubed up his finger and the thermometer before he circled her anus with his finger.

Charlotte stiffened, and her eyes shot open.

"Daddy!" she screamed.

Both men flinched, and Finn was quick to give Charlotte his hand so she could mess around with it.

"Play with Daddy's hands while Michael takes your

temperature," he said. "Be a good girl for Daddy, and don't wiggle around too much."

Tears of frustration formed in her eyes and fell down her cheek as she held onto his hand.

"Play with Daddy's hands," he encouraged her.

Next time this happened, he would bring her stuffie, Moody, over so she could hug and snuggle up against him. He should've thought about that for this time, but he was so concerned about her health that it slipped his mind.

Charlotte started to squirm a little, and her face got flush. What was she thinking? Finn wanted to ask her, but he didn't want to embarrass her anymore than she already felt. He would have to ask later when they were alone.

"Just a couple more minutes, and then we're done," Michael said.

Charlotte started to play with his fingers, and he was thankful she relaxed some. He knew it was uncomfortable, but it was for her health, and that was important.

"She has a slight fever right now. Can you tell me her symptoms?" Michael asked as he pulled the thermometer out of Charlotte. Finn placed her legs down on the changing table, and she relaxed more.

"She's exhausted, lethargic, warm but shivers, scratchy and hoarse voice, and it's achy all over," Finn described.

He had kept a close eye on her while he talked to her before they left her house. She didn't have to tell him how she felt because she was an open book at that moment. She didn't hide a thing. Probably because it was so exhausting.

"It sounds like a common cold right now. I want you to make sure she gets enough fluid, eats three meals a day with some snacks in between, and gets enough sleep," Michael said. "If she gets a fever, you can give her medicine. Snuggle her all she wants. If she doesn't get better in the next couple of days, then call me, and we'll run more tests to see what's wrong."

"Thank you again for coming this early. I really appreciate it," Finn said.

"Welcome. Next time I see you, little one, I expect you to be all better. It's no fun feeling icky, and I want to properly meet you."

Charlotte didn't look at him, but she nodded her head. Michael chuckled and headed toward the door.

"I'll let myself out," he said before he pulled something out of his bag and placed it on the table next to the crib. "Oh, wait, I suspected it might be a cold since it's that time of the year and brought medicine. The special medicine."

Finn couldn't help but smile at that. Special medicine was the code word for suppository medicine. He couldn't wait to give her some, feel her tight ring around his finger.

"Daddy?" Charlotte whispered.

He turned around and walked to her.

"You did so well for Daddy," he praised her.

"I did?" She looked at him with big eyes.

"You did, little cupcake. So well."

Relaxed, Charlotte closed her eyes and made grabby hands at Finn. His heart melted as she sought comfort, and he was going to give it to her.

Finn unfastened the restraints and picked her up. He walked over to the rocking chair and sat down, placing Charlotte bridal style on his lap. She immediately snuggled into his embrace as he started to rock.

"Daddy's here. You fall asleep," he whispered.

Charlotte brought a thumb up to her mouth and started to suck on it. Right now, Finn wished he was close to the crib to grab a pacifier, but he didn't want to jostle her. She was about to fall asleep, and he didn't want her to fight sleep if he tried to move.

Next time he would have a pacifier on him so she could use it.

Charlotte grabbed a fistful of his shirt with the other hand and snuggled closer to him.

"Daddy's got you," he soothed her.

Finn sat there for hours as he watched his little cupcake sleep in his lap, and it was the best time.

CHAPTER TWENTY-FOUR

FINN

A couple hours later, Charlotte was awake again. She was moody, tired, slightly hungry, and just wanted to be held. She had woken up and started to cry, but once Finn picked her up, she settled down some.

Charlotte just wanted to be cuddled, and he was going to give her all the cuddles she wanted.

Right now, Finn was going to give her medicine because he didn't after Michael had left. He had wanted to give her medicine, and should have, but thought against it because he didn't want to distress her anymore.

Granted, he should've done it right after Michael finished taking her temperature. That's what he should have done, but he didn't, so he was doing it now.

"Daddy's going to lay you on your side." He placed Charlotte down on the changing table.

Charlotte whined and tried to grab onto his shirt, but he softly withdrew her fingers and put the straps around her torso and legs. He didn't want her to fall off the changing table if she moved. Finn would be moving around, and he didn't want to take the chance of her rolling or trying to grab him and falling off. That would make her feel a lot worse, and who knows what injuries she would get.

Finn didn't think she realized that she didn't have any pants or underwear on, and he wasn't going to bring attention to it right now.

He wanted to get the medicine into Charlotte as soon as possible so that it started to work. They had gotten a temperature from her an hour ago, and she still had a fever.

"Daddy!" Her voice raised. "Daddy!"

"Shhh, it's alright, my little cupcake," he whispered to her as he ran his hands through her hair. "You're okay. It's just going to be a couple of minutes, and then you can be back in Daddy's arms."

Finn grabbed Moody and handed it to Charlotte. She immediately latched onto it and snuggled into him as he started to get the medicine. He didn't know how she was going to react, but he hoped he could move fast enough before she realized what was happening.

He wanted her healthy, and that meant giving her medicine through her bottom in case she threw up. Finn didn't want to give her medicine and then have her throw it up a couple minutes later.

Charlotte had complained about being nauseous when he took her temperature. Good thing Michael left suppositories and not the regular kind of medicine.

Finn grabbed the suppository and moved her knees up to her chest.

"Daddy?" she whispered half asleep.

"It's okay," he replied. "You're doing okay."

Finn was quick to line up the medicine and push it in.

199

"Daddy! Noooo!" Charlotte whined, fully awake now.

"You're okay. Just a minute and then it's all done," Finn said as he kept his finger in her bottom.

He didn't want to take the chance of her pushing it out. Finn already felt her trying to push it out.

"Take it out! Take it out!" she cried. "I don't want it. I'm all good!"

Finn held his finger there for a couple more seconds before he pulled it out. He kissed her forehead and let her legs relax.

"I'm going to go wash my hands. Be a good girl and lie still," Finn said.

He quickly washed his hands, not wanting to leave Charlotte there for too long by herself. The straps were there to keep her safe and on the table, but nothing was full proof, and he didn't want to take any chances.

"There's my good little cupcake!" he praised her when he walked back into the room.

"Pants, Daddy," she whimpered. "Pants on me."

Finn had thought about putting her in a diaper, but he didn't know if that was a hard limit or not. He hadn't asked her when they went over the contract, and he didn't want to just assume it was okay. What if it brought back bad memories and she had a panic attack?

Finn had thought about asking Charlotte right now, but he knew that she wasn't fully there because she didn't feel good. He would just have to keep a close eye on her until she felt better and he could ask her.

That would be taking advantage of the situation, and he didn't want to do that. He didn't want to do it and then regret it later because she didn't want it.

"Do you want Daddy's pants or your onesie?" Finn asked.

In the corner of her closet, he found a onesie that looked almost brand new. He didn't know if she had just gotten it or if she had placed it there and forgotten, but he brought it just in case.

This one didn't have a flap where the butt was, but he would be looking into some. It was better to have one with a flap at the bottom because it would give him easier access when she was naughty, and it would give her easy access if she needed to go to the bathroom.

While Charlotte took her nap later on, Finn was going to look and see if he could find any. He knew a couple of littles and caregivers that worked or created clothing for littles. He would have to contact one of them to see if he could get something made.

Finn had been meaning to talk to them anyway because they wanted to start selling clothes at the club, have their logo on some. They wanted to let the littles and caregivers be able to look around while they were in the club for things they need.

They had been wanting to do this for a couple of years, but they never got around to it until recently. It was another thing on Finn's list to do for the club, and now he just needed to find time.

Finn never thought that he was going to find a little for him, and so he threw himself into work and took on a lot because he had a lot of free time, but that was changed now. He'd found his little one, and he wanted to spend more time with her.

He started by asking Michael, Marco, and Mac if they could help out with some of his workload and maybe rearrange something. Maybe it was time for Finn to find a personal assistant that can help out with some of the less important things.

None of them had personal assistants, but he'd found his little one, and Mac had his eyes on a little girl, so they were going to start getting busy with their littles. He didn't want the club to suffer, so his next thing was to hire a personal assistant.

"Pants, Daddy," Charlotte whined.

Finn got pulled out of his thoughts, and he looked over at his little cupcake.

"Pants or onesie?" Finn asked again.

"Onesie!" she excitedly said before she started coughing.

"Inside voices, little cupcake. Especially since you're sick."

Charlotte pouted. He didn't like scolding her, especially when she was excited, but she was sick, and he didn't want her to overexert herself. She needed all the rest she could get, and getting wound up wasn't good right now.

Finn went and grabbed the onesie from the back before he walked over and unstrapped her. He had thought about grabbing underwear but thought against it. If she needed the bathroom in an emergency since she wasn't wearing a diaper, he didn't want to have another layer to take off since her onesie didn't have a drop seat.

"Underwear?" Charlotte whispered.

"Not today, little cupcake. In case of emergencies, you're not going to wear one right now," Finn explained.

"But—" she started to say.

"No buts," he replied. "Daddy knows best. We don't want you to make a mess in your panties. Your onesie doesn't have a drop seat, and if you really need to go, Daddy has to take off your onesie and pull it down."

"O-okay."

He helped Charlotte get dressed in her cute, little polka-dotted onesie before setting her on the ground. She immediately motioned her hands in a grabby way, indicating that she wanted to be picked up.

"Give Daddy one second," he said.

Charlotte let out a whine and made grabby hands again.

"Daddy."

"Charlie, Daddy said one second," he scolded her a little.

He knew she was sick, but she needed to know that when Daddy said one second, he meant to give him a little bit to finish what he was doing. He wasn't opposed to giving her a couple little swats on her bottom to remind her of that. He wouldn't give her a full blown punishment until she was fully better if she did anything wrong though, but he hoped it wouldn't come to that.

"Daddy knows that you're not feeling good, but that doesn't mean that you need to disobey," he said.

Finn grabbed one of the pacifiers next to the changing table and put it in his pocket. He picked up Charlotte and started to walk downstairs.

She needed fluid in her body. He had given her a bottle when she woke up, and she gladly drank from it.

Finn wasn't in her house long enough, but in her playroom, he didn't see any bottles or sippy cups that she drank out of. Maybe they were all in her kitchen, and he didn't see it.

Her kitchen.

She didn't have electricity, and he didn't know if she had

anything in her fridge that would go bad. He needed to go check on that, but he didn't want to leave her alone.

He also thought that she might not appreciate him going into her house. Maybe he could get Jaxson or Mac to go and see if anything needed to be thrown away. Finn didn't want her house to start to smell because food had gone bad.

Charlotte snuggled into his neck and relaxed some. He could get used to this if he wanted to. Fin wanted to always hold her.

"Daddy's gonna get you a bottle, and we'll sit in the rocking chair, and Daddy will feed you," Finn said as he started to fill up the bottle with chocolate milk.

Even though Charlotte was sick, he had seen her eyes light up earlier today when she saw the milk. Chocolate milk was good for her because it gave her protein, but it also gave her fluids. Charlotte didn't say anything but snuggled into his embrace more.

"Will you be Daddy's good little cupcake and drink all of it?" he asked.

He had given her water before in the bottle, and she didn't drink it all. He had to shake the bottle to get her attention and talk to her.

"Almost done, little cupcake," Finn whispered to her as he shook the bottle once again.

Her eyes slightly opened, and she let out a whine of protest.

"Be a good girl for Daddy, and drink the little bit that's left." Finn squeezed the bottle to encourage her to drink. Charlotte started to suckle the nipple and finished the rest of the bottle. "Good girl," he murmured to her. "Such a good girl for Daddy."

She nestled her face into his chest and relaxed as Finn started to rock them back and forth. They should make this a before nap time routine. He brought her comfort, but she also brought him comfort by letting him take care of her.

"Daddy," she mumbled and put her thumb in her mouth.

Finn was quick to act and grabbed the pacifier on the little table next to the rocking chair. He pulled her thumb out of her mouth, and before she could whine, he placed the pacifier in her mouth.

"Good girl," he said again.

She was such a good girl for him right now, and he wanted to remind her of that. Finn watched as Charlotte fell asleep in his arms before he got out of the rocking chair and placed her in the crib.

Charlotte let out a whine, but Finn was fast enough to place his hand on her stomach and gently rub it, putting her back to sleep. She sucked the pacifier harder and rolled to her side. Finn placed Moody right next to her, and she instantly grabbed it.

A smile broke out of his face at the act Charlotte made. She was so stinking cute when she was did those things, and he couldn't get enough of it.

With that last thought, he walked out of her room and to his computer. He was going to go shopping for her, spoil her while she napped.

CHAPTER TWENTY-FIVE

CHARLOTTE

*C*harlotte didn't know what was going on around her. She had been embarrassed the other day when one of Daddy's friends came over and checked her temperature. In her bottom.

How mortifying was it to have an adult man stick something in her bottom to check her temperature. His friend of all people. Now, whenever she saw him at the club, she wouldn't be able to look him in the eyes or even at him in general.

She knew her face was going to go beat read whenever she saw Michael next. Maybe she could slip away any time she saw a glance of him so she didn't have to interact with him. That sounded like a safe bet to her. Finn wouldn't approve, but he wasn't in her place. He didn't know how embarrassing it was to have her temperature checked in her bottom.

She never wanted that to happen to her again. It was embarrassing and humiliating for that to happen. Charlotte had felt a light bit of arousal when Michael moved the thermometer around in her bottom, and she was embarrassed. It was another man who was making her aroused and not her Daddy.

What would Daddy think if he found out about that? She tried so hard not to get turned on, but it was hard. The slight burn when Michael pushed the thermometer into her bottom turned her on, the stretching feeling as her hole clenched around the thermometer.

She knew Michael was an ex doctor, but that didn't make it any better. If anything, it made it worse. He was Daddy's friend but also an owner of the club.

Charlotte hated doctors and never wanted to see one again in her life. They scared her no matter how much they tried to tell her otherwise.

That was why Charlotte never went to the doctor unless it was an emergency, and that happened very rarely. She tried her best not to have to go to the doctor, but recently it had been slipping between her fingers, and she knew why.

Before, her health was a priority, but since she got the second job and was worried about her electric and water getting turned off, it hadn't been. She hadn't been eating as well as she would have liked, and she got less sleep.

Her health slipped through her fingers, pushed to the back and forgotten about. Charlotte knew it was only time before she had to go to the doctor again, but she was trying to make it a little longer.

And she wanted to go to a regular doctor, even though they were just as scary, because having Daddy's friend come over was a lot. He would see her everywhere if Daddy was around whereas if she went to a regular doctor, she wouldn't.

Charlotte knew that if they went to the club, Michael

would most likely be there, and he would say hi to her Daddy. How mortifying. Would other people know that he stuck a thermometer up her bottom to check her temperature?

She shook her head and pushed those thoughts away. She didn't need to be thinking about that because she knew if she did, it wouldn't end well. Happy thoughts were what Charlotte should be thinking about. How Daddy made her so happy and taken such good care of her while she was sick. He was such a good Daddy, and Charlotte knew she was lucky to have him.

Relaxed, Charlotte turned to her side and looked between the crib bars. She still felt icky, but it was better than it had been. He had been giving her some type of medicine in her bottom the past two nights, and it had done wonders. Or maybe it was the sleep she had gotten.

Daddy had made sure she got enough sleep at night and took naps during the day. The first day she didn't fight the naps or the early bedtime, but yesterday she had, and she got a warning from her Daddy.

She hadn't fought on going to bed early because by that time she was exhausted and just wanted to snuggle up to her Daddy and fall asleep. When she took naps in the day, Daddy would put her in the crib, but at night she would sleep in his bed with him.

It was hard last night, even though she was sleepy. Charlotte had always felt physically attracted to her Daddy, but it wasn't until she got into his bed that it grew. Yes, she had some fantasies about him and what he would do to her, but being in his arms in his bed only increased them.

Charlotte had woken up this morning with wet panties,

and it wasn't from pee. She was mortified and ran to the bath-room to clean herself up. She didn't know what came over her last night, but she hoped Finn didn't find out.

Her underwear did have to be changed, and she threw them into the dirty clothes bin before she walked downstairs and had breakfast with Finn. That's when she got scolded for walking down the stairs when she was sick.

Charlotte had also gotten a talk about getting out of bed without Daddy's help. She had given the excuse that she really needed to go to the bathroom, but she didn't think he bought it. He just told her that, next time, she should wake him up and have him help her out of the bed safely.

She wanted to argue, but she didn't. Charlotte vaguely remembered him telling her he wasn't afraid of giving her a couple swats on her bottom to remind her who was in charge. Her bottom tingled with that though, and she knew she got turned on by it.

Having his hands on her bottom? Heaven, but she knew he wasn't talking about making her feel good. It was a punish-ment, and punishments were supposed to hurt.

Daddy said he wanted to talk to her about something for when she took a nap or was going to sleep for a long time, but she couldn't think of what it could be. He wanted to wait until after her second nap to talk about it. That should be any time now.

Now Charlotte had woken up from her second nap and was waiting for her Daddy to come and get her. He told her that he had a monitor with video and sound to watch over her while she slept. That if she needed anything, he would be able to tell and come right away.

That comforted her, and she had fallen asleep a lot easier

for her nap. She still fought when she fell asleep because she didn't need to take naps anymore. She felt a lot better than she did two days ago when Daddy picked her up from her house.

Charlotte groaned at that thought. He had called her out of work from both jobs, today and tomorrow since she was sick. Both employers understood and just wanted her to get better. They even gave her three extra days because they wanted her to get fully better before coming back. Did Finn say something to make them say that or were they just that kind?

Charlotte didn't know if it was paid or not, and that worried her. She needed the money and didn't know if she could wait four more days until she went back to work. That was a lot of money that she could have had.

They still hadn't had the conversation about her working two jobs yet, and she wasn't looking forward to that conversation. She knew she had to tell him the truth, and she was prepared to, but she wasn't prepared for the punishments she earned.

Getting a second job had made her health suffer, and that was one of his rules. She already had a punishment for not getting enough sleep each night, and she didn't want to add any more on to that.

But she knew she was going to. She lied about multiple things, didn't come to him when she knew she should have, and broke his trust a little. Everything she felt guilty for and had for a while. The tight knot in her stomach grew and weighed heavy.

Daddy was going to be so disappointed when he knew

everything, and she didn't know if she could handle that. She didn't want to disappoint her Daddy, but it seemed like she just kept doing it.

Would he want to get rid of her after he found everything out? She hoped not, but she needed to be prepared for that. Daddy could very well tell her he didn't want her anymore since he couldn't trust her to come to him for things or not lie.

That would break her heart, but she would have to suck it up. Well, Charlotte could beg for forgiveness, and she would. She would tell him how guilty she felt and that if he'd still have her, she'd be a better baby girl for him.

"How's Daddy's precious little cupcake doing?" Daddy's voice filled the room and brought her out of her thoughts.

Charlotte's heartbeat increased with his voice. Oh, she loved it when he spoke to her, called her his little cupcake, and held her. It made her tummy have butterflies in it, and she loved that feeling.

Her mind had been a lot clearer today, and she knew they were going to talk about things. Was she ready for that, or should she pretend like she still didn't feel good?

If she pretended, it could go two ways. She would gets out of the conversations and nothing happened. Or he'd get even more worried and take her to the emergency room, and she would get out of the conversation.

Charlotte didn't know if she wanted to play with fate and have to go to the emergency room, explaining that she was fine or keep pretending so the doctors say that she was fine.

"Better," she whispered, feeling out of breath.

Daddy's face came into her view, and it was concerned.

"Why are you out of breath? Are you okay? Having trouble breathing? Do I need to call Michael and get you checked again?" He fired off questions.

Her face turned red, and she pulled Moody up to cover it. How was she supposed to tell him she was out of breath from thinking about him and how much he turned her on when he walked into the room?

"Little cupcake, you can tell me anything," Daddy said as he rubbed her back.

Charlotte peaked around Moody to see his face. He still looked concerned but less than he did before.

"Embarrassed," she whispered before she smushed her face into Moody again. Would he be turned off because she was turned on by him? Did he only want a little girl and nothing sexual? Did he only see her as a little girl, or did he also see her as the woman she was?

"Little cupcake," Daddy said. "You know you don't have to be embarrassed to tell Daddy, right? There's nothing between Daddy and his little cupcake."

Charlotte kept her face in Moody. Embarrassment flooded her body.

"Cupcake." He placed his hand on her back and rubbed it. "Does this have anything to do with the underwear I found in the dirty hamper?"

She gasped and looked at him. He found the underwear? Her face turned beat red before she covered her face with Moody again. How embarrassing. He found her soaked underwear.

"Charlotte," he called out. "Can you look at me?"

She shook her head. She didn't want to look at him right

now, not when he knew her secret. How was she going to explain what that was? Would he believe it if she told him she had wet herself?

"Cupcake, please look at me."

It was hard for Charlotte not to look at him when he talked to her like that. His voice was so sweet but commanding at the same time. It made her want to obey him, no matter what.

Charlotte turned over and peaked from behind Moody.

"There's my beautiful little cupcake." A smile broke out across his face.

Daddy ran his hands through Charlotte's hair and helped her relax some.

"Daddy did some laundry today while you were napping and found your underwear. You didn't have an accident, did you? I didn't find anything on the bed to indicate you did."

Charlotte shook her head. She was caught red handed, and she couldn't lie about it. He knew what it was, and there was no way around it.

"Words, little cupcake," Daddy got onto her.

Charlotte knew he liked words; that was another one of the rules, well, lesser rules. Daddy always wanted a verbal answer, and she tended to forget. It was something she was trying to work on, but she still forgot.

"No, Daddy. I didn't wet myself," she whispered.

"I think I have an idea of what it was, but could you tell me?" he asked.

Charlotte's mouth went dry. If he already knew, why did she have to say it out loud?

"It's okay, you can do it," Finn encouraged her.

"I was turned on," she replied.

"Turned on by what?"

Charlotte's face went red, and she tried to hide it, but he wouldn't let her. He cupped her cheek and held her head in place.

"You can tell Daddy."

"You."

Satisfaction filled his face, and he kissed her forehead.

"Daddy's pleased to hear that," he murmured against her skin.

Charlotte stared at him in shock. Daddy was pleased?

"Daddy is so pleased to hear that," he said. "Daddy's little cupcake is so beautiful."

She blushed and looked away from him. Charlotte hadn't been called beautiful in a long time, and she found it weird. Did she just say thank you and move on?

"Daddy is so pleased to see that you feel the same way he does. You don't have to hide anything from Daddy," he said. "Daddy wants to know when you're turned on by him, so he can take care of you."

Charlotte looked at him. He wanted her to tell him when she was turned on so he could take care of her? Was he a real person right now? She didn't know if she would be able to tell him when she was turned on.

That would be so embarrassing to let him know. What if she was always turned on? What if she was turned on when he spanked her?

Charlotte had heard of other littles getting turned on when they got spanked, and she didn't know how to respond to that.

"I know it might be hard in the beginning, but you'll get used to it."

She didn't know if she would get used to it or not.

He held her hands and rubbed the back of them with his thumb.

"Charlotte, I think since you're feeling better we need to have a serious conversation."

CHAPTER TWENTY-SIX

CHARLOTTE

*N*erves ran through her body when Daddy said he wanted to talk to her. Was this when he was going to tell her he didn't want anything to do with her?

Why would he give a whole speech about her underwear and not having to hide anything and then tell her he didn't want her anymore? It didn't make sense, but anything could happen at this point.

"Cupcake," Daddy called out. "I need you to stop thinking whatever you're thinking."

Charlotte made eye contact with him and nodded her head. It would be hard, but she would try. At this point, Charlotte had sat up in her crib with her feet dangling, and Daddy was sitting in a small chair in front of her.

What could he want to talk about, then? Could it be because she got a second job and she didn't let him know? Could it be because she put her health in danger and that was a major rule?

"We need to have a serious discussion, and I think we can have it today because you're feeling better," he said.

Could she make up that she started to feel worse right now? Would he believe it or call her bluff? Charlotte thought for a second before she decided against it. He would know if she lied, and she didn't want to add onto the punishment if he was going to talk about that.

They stared at each other for a while before Daddy spoke again.

"Why didn't you tell me you got another job? Why didn't you tell Daddy that you were struggling?" he asked. "Daddy would've helped you out in any way you needed."

She knew he would, and that's what she was worried about. They hadn't known each other long, and he was ready to give her anything and everything, and that scared her.

Was this normal for a guy to do that, or was it just him? Had he done this before?

Charlotte shrugged her shoulders, but she knew why. She was embarrassed, and she didn't want to be a charity case. She worked hard to earn her money, and she didn't want to mooch off of someone.

If she had told Daddy about her struggling, he would've paid for things. He would've told her that he could take care of her every need. She wanted that, but she also didn't want to mooch off of him. They hadn't been together long, and she didn't want to rely on him financially so early into their relationship.

Would he think of her less for that? Would he realize just how poor she was and not want anything to do with her anymore?

Charlotte wanted to give up all control and let him take care of everything, but she didn't want to be a burden. He had worked hard over the years for that money, and she didn't want to just take it.

"Cupcake, don't shrug your shoulders when you know the answer," Daddy said as if he could tell that Charlotte knew the real reason.

She looked down at her hands and started to play with them. The only thing she could do right now was play with them. She knew that he would make her look at him soon. Daddy liked for her to look him in the eyes when she talked.

"You can tell me anything. I won't be mad or make fun of you. Daddy wants you to be able to come to him for anything and everything."

Taking a deep breath, Charlotte looked up at her Daddy and nodded her head. She could do this. He had told her so many times that she didn't need to be embarrassed or afraid to tell him anything. That he would be supportive and try to help her out, and she was starting to believe him.

Daddy had told her so many times, and when she did talk to him about something, he always listened to her and made her feel like she was the only person in the world at that moment. He made her feel special and giddy inside.

"I was embarrassed and didn't want to be a charity case," she whispered.

Everything inside of her screamed for her to run to the bathroom and hide from her Daddy, but his hand on her knee stopped her. His touch calmed her a little bit, but she still felt jittery and nervous about what he was going to say.

"Daddy didn't hear. Can you say it a little louder?" he asked.

She stared at him with wide eyes before she recoiled. Did

he really not hear, or did he just want her to admit it again? Did he get off on embarrassing her?

Charlotte didn't know if she could deal with that. She didn't like to be embarrassed or humiliated. It never made her feel good, and she always tried to avoid it.

"Daddy really didn't hear. You were so quiet. Daddy would never make fun of you by asking you to repeat something," he said and calmed some of her worry.

"I was embarrassed and didn't want to be a charity case," Charlotte said again but louder this time.

Daddy stared at her and blinked a couple of times. Worry filled Charlotte, and before she knew it, she was speaking again.

"W-we just started our relationship, and I didn't want to rely on you financially. I k-knew that once you found out..." Charlotte took a breath. "I knew, I knew that."

Daddy placed his other hand on her knee and gave it a little squeeze.

"Breath," he encouraged her. "Big breath. Good girl. Another one. Such a good girl."

Charlotte relaxed, and her brain became less fuzzy.

"Now, what were you saying?" he asked.

She was grateful he wasn't just going to forget that she was talking before. Charlotte had several guys who, once she took a breath to regain her composure, would start talking and completely forget that she was.

"I knew that once you found out I needed help financially, you would step in. I was embarrassed that you would hate me for having to help me out. I didn't earn the money, so I didn't want you to spend it on my bills that were overdo."

Charlotte had finally gotten it out, and a little weight

219

came off her shoulders, but at the same time, it didn't. She was glad she finally told her Daddy about it, but she was worried he would be disappointed in her.

"Charlotte," Daddy started to say. "I want you to pay close attention to what I'm about to say. Can you do that for Daddy?"

She nodded her head but quickly spoke. "Yes, Daddy."

"Good girl."

Charlotte relaxed more. He didn't sound angry or disappointed right now.

"Daddy wants you to know that he would never hate you for needing help with paying bills. Daddy would never hate you for anything; it's not possible," he said as he ran his hands up and down her thigh. "You don't need to be embarrassed about needing help financially either, and you aren't a burden. Daddy loves to take care of you. It makes him feel wanted."

Charlotte hung onto his words like they were her lifeline. Every word he spoke calmed her down more and more.

"Daddy loves it when you come to him for things. It makes him feel like you trust him with things," he said. "He knows you may not come to him with things right away, but he hopes you know that you can eventually come to him for things. And you aren't a charity case, never in Daddy's eyes. People go through struggles in life every now and the, and that's okay."

Her eyes started to water as he continued to talk.

"Daddy had to ask Jaxson for help with money several years ago. It's okay to ask for help, and it doesn't make you weak. You are so strong, but you don't have to do it alone.

Daddy is here to catch you, to take care of you, and to love you."

Charlotte flung herself at her Daddy. Everything he said was so sweet, and she believed it.

"I've got you," he whispered into her ear. "Daddy meant every word he said."

She nodded her head in his shoulder and continued to hold onto him. She didn't want to let him go, not after he told her all of those things.

Daddy pulled away from Charlotte and looked into her eyes.

"What you did though still broke rules. You put your health in danger, and you knew it. You also didn't sleep a minimum of eight hours. You lied to Daddy when you said you had a project going on," he listed off.

Her shoulders started to sag with each mention of the things she did wrong, the rules she broke.

"All of those deserve a spanking," he said, and Charlotte gasped.

She shook her head. Maybe she could do corner time instead.

"I'm still not one hundred percent better," she whispered, hoping it would get her out of the spanking.

"Not getting out of the spanking. If you want, we can wait until you get better, but for every day that goes by, I'll be adding more spankings."

Charlotte's eyes went wide with that news. She didn't know how many spankings she was going to get or how many he would add if she waited.

"So what's it going to be?" Daddy asked.

"Spankings now," she mumbled.

He pulled away from Charlotte. He quickly kissed her nose before setting her feet on the ground and stood up.

"I'm proud of you," he said as he sat on the bigger chair in the corner.

Charlotte stood where she was, not knowing if she should walk to him or stay in place. Daddy hadn't called her over to him or told her she could move, and she didn't want to add any more punishments on to what she already had.

"Good girl for staying there. Come to Daddy now," he said.

Charlotte dragged her feet as she walked to her Daddy. How many spankings would he give her? She hoped it wasn't a lot, but who didn't hope that?

"Daddy's going to take off your onesie now and spank you." Daddy started to unzip her onesie.

She didn't fight him on this, and it took everything in her not to. Charlotte knew that if she said anything, he would say Daddy was supposed to take care of his little and that he could do it. There wasn't any point in trying to tell him she could do it herself.

"Hold on to Daddy's shoulders as you step out of it." He guided her hands to his shoulders.

She gripped onto them as he pushed her onesie down and off of her legs. Wind hit Charlotte's skin, and she felt so exposed. She let go of his shoulders and covered her boobs with her arms.

"Did Daddy say you could let go of his shoulders?" he asked as he stared into her eyes after he placed Charlotte's onesie on the little table.

She shook her head and hesitantly placed her hands back

on his shoulders. She felt so exposed in front of him. She was fully naked, and he had all of his clothes on.

She started to get turned on with the thought of seeing him naked. When would she see him fully naked?

"Ready for your spanking?" Daddy asked.

Charlotte nodded her head, but inside she wasn't ready. Was anyone ever ready for a spanking?

"Crawl onto my lap, and we'll get started."

She followed his direction and crawled onto his lap, getting into position. Even though she had only been in this position once when they first met, she remembered. How could she forget?

"I'm going to give you twenty hard spankings, and you're going to count after every one," Daddy said. "Harder than the first time I spanked you. And remember to keep your hands in front of you the whole time."

"Yes, Daddy," she whispered.

Charlotte was nervous about this punishment. She thought that the last spanking she got from him was bad, and he said it was going to be harder? Would her bottom be bruised by the end of this?

Without any sort of warning, Finn started to spank her. Fiery pain spread across her bottom a couple seconds after. Charlotte held in her yelp.

"One. Thank you, Daddy."

"Such a good girl saying thank you to her Daddy."

Charlotte blushed and wiggled in his lap. She couldn't help but be turned on as the pain turned into pleasure.

Smack.

Daddy hit her other cheek harder, and Charlotte let out a noise of protest. Everything was hurting worse than it had before. Would she be able to make it through the whole thing?

"Two. Thank you, Daddy."

The spankings continued to get harder and harder as Finn dished out the punishment. By the end, Charlotte was in tears.

"T-twenty." Charlotte took a gasping breath after a sob broke past her mouth. "T-thank you, D-daddy."

She went limp in his lap and tried to get her mind off of her bottom that hurt so bad, but the guilt in her stomach had gone away. It ached and it throbbed as Charlotte continued to cry.

She slowly calmed down, and she couldn't deny how turned on she was. While it did hurt after each spanking, she had felt the arousal build up.

Daddy pulled her upright and placed her on his lap, holding her close to him.

"Daddy's so proud of you. You took your punishment so well," Daddy praised her.

Charlotte blushed and buried her head into his chest. She felt herself starting to get wetter as he praised her and held her close. The proximity to him, the ache between her legs, and the throb on her bottom all turned her on.

She started to squirm in his lap, trying to get some pleasure, but her Daddy was fast to stop that.

A small swat landed on her bottom, and Charlotte let out a little yell.

"Noooo," she drawled out and tried to move again.

"Little girls that just got punished don't get to come after," Daddy said.

"But Daddy," Charlotte whined. "I need to come."

"Sorry, little cupcake. No pleasure after a punishment, and if I find out that you pleasured yourself and came, you'll get an even worse punishment," he said. "Do you understand?"

"Yes, Daddy."

Daddy set Charlotte down on the ground and stood up.

"Hungry?" he asked right as her stomach grumbled. Daddy chuckled and grabbed her hand. "Let's go feed the tummy monster."

CHAPTER TWENTY-SEVEN

CHARLOTTE

*H*ours had passed since Charlotte got her punishment, and the ache between her legs still hadn't gone away.

"Cupcake, I want to talk to you about something." Daddy walked into the living room where she was coloring on the floor.

Charlotte looked up at her Daddy to see that he had stopped.

"What, Daddy?" she asked.

"Such a precious girl. My precious little cupcake looking so cute coloring on the floor," he said as he walked toward her.

Worry filled her as daddy didn't say anything about what he wanted to talk to her about. Was he trying to deflect what he really wanted to talk about?

Daddy sat down on the floor right next to her and placed his hand on her back. She had been lying on her tummy for a while now.

"Can you sit up for Daddy?" he asked.

Charlotte set up and criss-crossed her legs. She gave him her full attention.

"I wanted to try this when you were sick, but I didn't know if it was a hard limit or not. I didn't want to do anything without knowing first, but since you're feeling better, I want to ask."

What could he possibly want to know? He gave no clue of what he was wanting to talk about in what he just said.

"While you were sick, I helped you to go to the bathroom several times. You were so out of it, so I don't know if you remember or not," he said.

Charlotte remembered alright. She wanted to forget that it happened. It was so embarrassing for him to be in the bathroom while she went and then to clean up after her.

It was weird and she didn't know if she liked it. It wasn't a hard limit for sure, but it was weird.

"While you were sick, I thought about diapering you up so that I didn't have to hold your shoulders while you went to the bathroom."

He wanted to diaper her up? He wanted her to use a diaper and then clean up after her?

Charlotte went to open her mouth, but daddy stopped her.

"And before you say that it's embarrassing and that you could never do it, have you ever worn one?" he asked.

Charlotte went to say yes, so she could get out of it, but quickly stopped to herself. She had thought about using diapers a year ago, but she didn't have anybody to clean up after herself, and she felt like if she used it, she should be in a younger headspace.

She didn't want to risk being in a younger headspace by herself. It was risky and could end badly.

"No," she whispered.

"Have you wanted to try one?"

Charlotte took a breath in. She knew it was a safe place to tell her Daddy that she had always wanted to try and wear a diaper, but it was hard. Charlotte had never admitted to anyone that she wanted to try one.

"Yes," she mumbled and looked down at her hands.

"Can you look at me, little cupcake?"

Charlotte looked up at her Daddy.

"Were you afraid to use one, or are you still afraid to use one?"

She nodded her head because it was the truth. She was afraid to use one before she met him because no one was there to take care of her.

"Can you tell me why?"

This was her time to tell him that she thought she was in a younger head space, but something stopped her.

Would he still want her if she was a younger Little?

"It's okay to tell Daddy anything," he encouraged her.

Charlotte took a deep breath. She could do this.

"I think I'm a younger little," Charlotte looked at her hands again.

Nerves ran through her body as she waited for him to say something. They hadn't talked about that yet, and she was nervous. Would he say no to her? Charlotte couldn't think of a reason why since he was the one that brought up her wearing a diaper.

She really needed to stop thinking of the worst, but it was

hard for her. She didn't have a lot of friends, and it was hard for her to connect with people and trust them right off the bat. It had always been that way for her.

Charlotte was always different, and people didn't want to be her friend. And if they did, it was never genuine. They just wanted to say they made friends with the weird girl and humiliated her.

"Cupcake, look at Daddy," he commanded.

She looked up to find him closer to her.

"Little one, I want you to know that it's okay if you think you're a younger little." He cupped her cheek with his hand. "Daddy is okay with that, and he wants you to be okay with that. I don't want you to be ashamed because you think you're younger. Be proud and comfortable because it's who you are."

Tears filled Charlotte's eyes, and she sniffled several times to keep them at bay. She didn't want to cry again, but his sweet words just made her melt.

"Daddy wants you to be so confident in yourself."

She nodded her head because she agreed with him. Charlotte had always wanted to be more confident in herself, but it never worked by herself. Maybe with her Daddy's help, she could become more confident.

"Now, do you still want to try one out or do you not anymore?" he asked.

"I w-want to try one," she whispered.

She had always wanted to try, and Charlotte didn't think it would ever go away. But she knew she would be embarrassed when Daddy changed her and cleaned her up because she would be exposed to him.

Like she was exposed to him earlier today when he gave her the spanking. Charlotte still felt the sting anytime she sat on the ground. That's why she colored on her stomach, so she didn't have to feel the pressure on her bottom.

It was also comfortable to lie on her stomach and color. It made her feel little, and she wanted that right now. She wanted the comfort of knowing that her Daddy would take care of everything while she colored.

"Do you want to try one now?"

Charlotte's eyes went wide with his question. She didn't think Daddy would suggest she put on one now. But if she didn't do it now, would she do it later?

"O-okay. You can give me the diaper, and I'll go put it on."

Daddy's face went serious, and he shook his head.

"Little girls don't put on or take off diapers by themselves. Daddy always helps," he said as he stood up from the ground.

Charlotte didn't think he would put it on, just clean up after her when she had used it, if she used it. She didn't even know if she would be able to use it. It was a foreign concept to wet herself and not be on the toilet.

Would it be easy and come naturally for her? Or would it be hard, and Charlotte had to think about it as she went?

"Hold Daddy's hand."

Charlotte placed her hand in his, and he helped her up from the ground. They walked together to the nursery and toward the changing table. Nerves flooded through Charlotte's body as her Daddy helped her up on the changing table and placed the straps around her body to keep her secure.

Every time Daddy put the straps around her, Charlotte couldn't help but feel secure and also turned on. Charlotte thought about the things he would do to her if he had his way with her.

Daddy pulled her pants and underwear down and neatly set them to the side.

"Do you trust Daddy?" he asked.

"Yes."

"Daddy's going to shave you real quick. It's not good to wear a diaper with hair. The hair just traps moisture, and it can end badly."

Charlotte didn't know how it could end badly, but he was Daddy and she wasn't, so she didn't really have to worry about it.

Daddy left the room, and a couple minutes later he came back with supplies in his hands.

"Spread your legs," he said as he sat everything down on the changing table.

Charlotte spread her legs and closed her eyes. She didn't want to see him get all close and personal to her. She knew she was already starting to get turned on.

Would he be able to tell?

Charlotte quickly closed her legs. She didn't want Daddy to know that she was turned on by the straps and the thought of him shaving her.

"Little cupcake," Daddy said.

Charlotte peaked her eyes open to see him giving her a disapproving look.

"Why did you shut your legs?"

Her face went bright red, and she looked at his chest instead of his eyes.

"Tell Daddy now."

"I s-started to get turned on," she mumbled quietly.

Silence filled the room, and Charlotte looked up at his face. Satisfaction filled his face, and Charlotte was taken back. He was glad?

"Daddy's happy you told him the truth. Daddy's also happy he can turn you on."

Charlotte's face got redder at his words. She felt at ease when he didn't comment about her speaking quietly or anything negative about her getting turned on.

"Now, open your legs for Daddy. If you're a good girl, maybe I'll give you a treat." He wiggled his eyebrows at her.

Charlotte immediately opened her legs and let her Daddy start to clip and then shave her hair. It felt weird the whole time to have him so close to her but not do anything.

"Such a good girl for Daddy," he commented as he continued to shave her.

She continued to relax as time went on and tried to think about anything else but her Daddy so close to her pussy. She knew he could tell she was turned on; she could feel it.

"Cupcake," Daddy said, and she looked at him. "Daddy doesn't want you to shave your pussy by yourself. It's always Daddy's job to do this. I don't want you to accidentally cut yourself. Do you understand?"

"Yes, Daddy."

He got back to work, finishing shaving her pussy and wiping away the shaving cream. Charlotte got lucky with the Daddy she had. He was so kind and took great care of her.

"All done." Daddy leaned down and kissed the top of Charlotte's pussy.

A gasp left her lips at the contact, and her back arched. It felt so good, and Charlotte wanted more.

"Please," she whimpered.

"You were such a good girl for Daddy. I think you need a reward," he said.

Charlotte nodded her head furiously, and Daddy chuckled. Without warning, Daddy went down and started to suck on her clit, teasing it every once in a while with his teeth.

"Oooohhhh," Charlotte breathed out as pleasure coursed through her body.

Daddy's fingers trailed higher and higher up her thigh as he continued to suck on her pussy. Her back arched, but the strap around her kept her mostly in place. His fingers lightly trailed against her pussy before they plunged in.

Pressure and pleasure built up inside of Charlotte as Daddy slowly pumped his finger into her.

"Please," she whispered after a moan escaped past her lips. "I need to come."

The pleasure was getting to become too much, and Charlotte knew she was close.

"Come whenever you want," Daddy said against her pussy before he got back to sucking and teasing her.

His teeth lightly bit down on her clit, sending her over the edge. Charlotte screamed as she came on his fingers. Everything around her was fuzzy as she came down from her orgasm.

Charlotte felt something being placed around her waist before the straps around her body were loosened and hands picked her up.

"Such a good girl," Daddy whispered in her ear as he

held her. "Just rest while Daddy takes care of you. I'm right here and not going anywhere."

Charlotte relaxed in his embrace, and Daddy started to rock them back and forth. She could get used to this, and she couldn't wait until this was her everyday life.

CHAPTER TWENTY-EIGHT

CHARLOTTE

Charlotte had to go back to work today, and she wasn't looking forward to it. She had felt better yesterday, but Daddy wanted to make sure she was one hundred percent okay before she went back to work.

She was worried about the bakery. What did they do without her? Who baked all the goodies? Were they better than what she made?

Charlotte wasn't worried about the other job because she asked for her hours to be cut back. It wasn't her first choice, but Daddy and Charlotte had a long conversation, and that was what they agreed upon.

Daddy wanted her to quit it completely, but Charlotte didn't want to depend on him too much. Well, that wasn't fully true. She still felt bad about taking his money without working for it. She felt like a charity case, even though he had told her several times that she wasn't.

He had told her he would help her out with her bills right now as she got back onto her feet. That she didn't need to worry about those things. Charlotte was glad, but she was also worried.

What if something happened and he didn't want her to be his little girl anymore? Would she have to repay him for all the bills he paid?

"Cupcake, stop thinking about that," Daddy said as he walked into the room.

It was too early, but Daddy insisted he wake up with her. She was groggy and just wanted to go back to sleep, but she promised James that she would come in today. James sounded relieved, but she wasn't one hundred percent sure.

"You can go back to sleep. I'm almost ready to go to work," Charlotte said.

She felt bad that he woke up with her. He didn't have to be awake for several more hours, but he decided that he was going to wake up with her.

"I'm not going back to sleep, and you can't change my mind." He gave her a look, and she closed her mouth.

Don't mess with Daddy so early in the morning, she noted in her brain for future references.

"Little cupcake, do you know that you're it for me? You're my little girl, my little precious cupcake. No one else will compare to you. I don't want anyone else but you," he said. "Stop worrying about me getting rid of you because it isn't happening. You're mine forever."

Charlotte nodded and relaxed her body. She believed him, but her thoughts always got the best of her, and he knew that. He constantly reminded her, and she wondered if he would get annoyed with that.

"W-will you get annoyed with reminding me?" she whispered and looked up at him.

"No, little cupcake. I won't ever get annoyed or tired of reminding you that you're mine forever and that there isn't anyone else."

She let out a sigh and wrapped her arms around his waist. She had to leave in a couple of minutes, but she wanted to spend a couple seconds in his arms.

"When is your break today?" Daddy asked and stood back from her.

Charlotte shrugged her shoulders. She didn't know when she would have a break. Sometimes she didn't get one because they were so busy, and she needed to bake all of the time.

"Do you not have a set break time?" he asked.

She shook her head. "No, I don't. It depends on how busy we are. It changes, and sometimes I don't get a break at all."

"I don't like that. Maybe I'll be having a discussion with James about that. It's not healthy to not have a break to eat and drink something."

"I do eat," Charlotte protested.

She did, but it might not be healthy like he would like.

"All sugary stuff. You need healthy things for snacks and a lunch. Do you ever eat lunch?"

Charlotte thought back to all the times she had worked at the bakery. Had she ever eaten lunch? Maybe in the very beginning but once the bakery got more known around the city, it was hard for her to take breaks.

"In the beginning. I haven't in a while. I just eat after my shift."

"And what do you normally eat after your shift?"

Charlotte moved around uncomfortably. She knew he wouldn't like the answer, but that's all she could afford at the time. She wasn't able to get the good stuff because it was so expensive.

"Beans and maybe some rice," she whispered.

"Well, that's going to change. Daddy's going to bring you lunch today, and you'll be taking a break to eat it. No ifs, buts, or ors. You'll be eating with me. A healthy lunch because you need it."

She nodded her head. Charlotte didn't want to argue with her Daddy right now. Not this early in the morning and not right before she had to leave him.

She felt giddy inside that he was taking care of her. It made her feel at ease and not worry as much. He had her best interest for her, and she liked it. She craved it.

"I'll see you for lunch," Daddy said as he kissed her forehead.

Charlotte grabbed her keys and purse and made her way outside of his house. It was still dark outside, and a little whine escaped past her lips. It was so hard for Charlotte to get out of her Daddy's bed this morning.

All she wanted to do was snuggle into his side and never leave, but she knew she had a job to do. She had been gone long enough, and they needed her back, or, well, she hoped they needed her back.

Charlotte didn't know what she would do if they didn't need her, but from the way James talked on the phone, they needed her back.

"Drive safe, and text me when you get there," Daddy said as he helped Charlotte into her car.

"Yes, Daddy. I will."

He closed the door, and Charlotte went on her way to

work. The whole ride to the bakery was a blur, and before she knew it, she was in the bakery turning the ovens on.

Charlotte quickly sent a text to her Daddy before she got to baking things.

"I'm so glad you're back!" Amelia yelled as she walked into the kitchen. "We had a replacement baker, but they weren't the same, and our customers noticed."

Charlotte felt bad for leaving them in a pickle when she got sick, but she was glad to hear that they were happy for her to be back. The worry went away, and pride filled her chest. Her customers noticed that it wasn't her baking.

"What are you making today?" Amelia asked.

"The usuals right now. Cupcakes, brownies, cookies, lemon squares."

"Ooooo I want some! Tell me when they come out, and I'll 'sample' them for you to see if they're good."

Before Charlotte could say anything, James walked right behind Amelia and grabbed her arm.

"She will do no such thing. I already told you today that you don't get any treats, and if I find out you ate some, then your punishment will be worse," James said, and Amelia pouted.

Charlotte went back to stirring some of the cupcake batter together. She needed to get them in the oven as soon as possible so she could let them start to cool. She didn't want another melting icing incident.

"I'm glad you're back and feeling better," James told Charlotte. "Your Daddy called and said he was coming for lunch. When he gets here, finish up whatever you were doing, and then go eat with him."

"Yes, sir."

James and Amelia left Charlotte to herself as she baked and got all the goodies together before they opened. Charlotte had always left when the bakery closed, but she wondered whether she stayed a couple hours after to bake some things if she would have less baking to do the next day.

Charlotte didn't know if James would allow her to do it or if it was even a wise idea. Maybe she could mention it to Daddy before she talked to James about it.

Hours had passed since she'd gotten to work, and she hadn't had a break yet. She was saving that for when Daddy came for lunch. Maybe she could have a little longer lunch with him instead of taking a break.

"Are those cupcakes okay to bring to the display?" Amelia peaked her head into the kitchen.

"Give me one second! I need to add the finishing touches before I bring them out."

Charlotte quickly added the sprinkles to the cupcakes and picked up the tray. When she moved to walk toward the front area, she felt her bladder make a presence again. She really needed to go several minutes ago and had completely forgotten about it.

"Here are the cupcakes," Charlotte said as she placed them down on the counter.

She didn't even wait for Amelia to say anything before she walked back into the kitchen. Amelia had a certain way she liked the display, and she wasn't going to encroach on her space.

Charlotte made sure everything was okay so she could go to the bathroom. The pressure increased in her bladder, and Charlotte took several deep breaths. She didn't know if she would be able to make it to the bathroom in time.

Her face got really red, and she crossed her legs. Charlotte had let herself get to this point several times when she was at her Daddy's house, but she had a diaper on, so it didn't matter because she went in the diaper.

Now she didn't have a diaper on, and she knew she couldn't make it to the bathroom. Tears sprung to her eyes as she felt herself starting to go to the bathroom. She stayed in her spot and grabbed her phone out of her back pocket and called her Daddy.

"Little cupcake," Daddy answered. "I'm about to leave the club to bring you lunch."

Charlotte didn't say anything but breathed heavily as she tried to keep her sobs down.

"Cupcake, what's wrong?"

"D-daddy," she whispered. "I h-had an accident."

A sob made it's way out of her mouth. She felt nasty just standing in her own urine. She didn't want to walk anywhere because then she would get it everywhere, but she didn't want to stay in her clothes. She wanted them off, and she wanted to become clean.

"It's okay. I've got some extra clothes with me. I'll be there in three minutes," Daddy said. "Where are you?"

"Kitchen."

"Stay where you are. No one will come into the kitchen until I get there. You're okay, cupcake."

She continued to cry silently and stood there waiting for

him to come. How could she have forgotten that she wasn't wearing a diaper?

"Cupcake, Daddy's here," he said as he walked into the kitchen.

One look at her and he quickly walked to her. He had a bag hanging from his shoulder. Daddy wrapped a hoodie around her waist, picked her up, and moved her to a different spot.

Charlotte watched as Daddy started to clean up her mess on the floor before he threw everything away and turned toward her.

"Let's go get you changed," he said as he picked her up.

"No." Her voice raised. "I'm dirty."

"Daddy doesn't care. Daddy just wants to get you all cleaned and then fed."

He carried her outside the bakery and into the backseat of his car. He gently placed her down on the covered back seats.

"The windows are tinted, and I placed something on the front window, so no one can see in," Daddy said as he started to pull her pants and underwear down.

Charlotte relaxed to her best ability, but it was weird. Would people really not be able to see them when they walked by? He had said they wouldn't, and she mostly believed him, but a little part of her felt like maybe it was possible.

Daddy cleaned her up and placed a diaper around her.

"Wait! Everyone will be able to tell that I'm wearing one," Charlotte said.

"No, they won't. You'll be wearing one of my shirts that'll cover it. No one will be able to tell. I promise."

When Daddy promised things, he meant it, and Charlotte knew that. Any time he made a promise, he always kept it.

"Now that you're all clean, let's go eat some lunch."

Charlotte held her arms up. Right now, she wanted to be held and comforted. It was embarrassing what happened in there, and she hoped no one else knew what happened. She wouldn't be able to show her face there if everyone knew that she had wet herself.

"No one knows besides your boss. I needed to make sure that no one walked into the kitchen before I got there, so he watched over the door. You're safe," Daddy said as he picked her up.

He grabbed a bag and closed the car door before he walked into the bakery again and toward the kitchen.

"I brought you a peanut butter and jelly sandwich with some snap peas, carrots, and a treat for after," Daddy said.

He went to let go of Charlotte, but she clung onto him.

"Not ready to let go of Daddy?" he asked.

"No," she whispered.

She wanted to be held by him for a little while longer. Charlotte wanted to feel safe, and he made her feel that way. He calmed the nerves that ran through her body.

"That's okay. Daddy will hold you while he feeds you."

Daddy sat down and placed Charlotte on her lap. She snuggled into his embrace and waited for him to get all of the food out.

Charlotte could get used to this. Sitting in his lap as he fed her, taking a break from work, and just being with him a lot.

"Just relax, and let Daddy take care of you for the next several minutes."

And that's what she did, and she loved every minute of it.

CHAPTER TWENTY-NINE

FINN

Several days had passed since Charlotte had the accident at the bakery. Finn had put a diaper on her every day before she went to work and would meet her for lunch where he would change it and feed her.

It was a nice routine they had, and he wanted that every day. Sadly, Charlotte had gone back to her house yesterday. Finn asked her several times to stay with him so he could take care of her, but she said she needed to go back.

That didn't sit well with him, but he didn't want to push her too far. They had introduced a lot since they first met, and it hadn't even been three months of them knowing each other. If anyone else looked into their relationship and time-line, they would say they were moving fast, but Finn felt like they were moving slow.

Finn had hoped that Charlotte would've been moved into his house by now, but she wasn't. She was holding back, and he didn't know why. Could it be that she still wanted that little piece of independence?

He had to remind himself that she had been on her

own for a while and never had a Daddy before. It was all new to her, and he couldn't blame her for being a little hesitant.

He had meant to talk to her about this several days ago, but he never had a good time to bring it up. There never was a good moment to talk about it, and he knew that. He just needed to bring it up and get it over with.

Finn wanted her to fully move in with him and not have anything hold her back. He wanted her fully and not with one foot out the door.

That's what he felt like it was.

One foot out the door, and if anything went wrong, she would bolt out the door and never turn back around.

He let out a sigh and leaned against the door to Charlotte's nursery. When she saw the nursery, her eyes brightened, and tears rolled down her face. She was so in love with it, and he had a hard time getting her out of there.

Charlotte's nap was almost over, and he knew he needed to get her up. She wouldn't sleep later tonight if he didn't.

She had gotten back from work and was absolutely exhausted. So Finn fixed her up a bottle, rocked her while she ate, and then placed her down for a nap. Charlotte didn't even complain, which meant she was exhausted.

He wondered if she got enough sleep last night. He wasn't there to make sure she actually went to sleep when she was supposed to, but she did message him goodnight. That didn't mean she went to bed at that time, but Finn wanted to believe that she did.

Finn walked into the room and over to her crib and stared at her. Charlotte had confided in him that she felt really small around him, and he knew exactly what she meant. She had some tendencies that were in younger littles, and he didn't mind.

Charlotte had been worried though. She had never explored that younger age because she didn't have anyone to take care of her in that vulnerable state. She didn't know if she would like it, and that's why Finn was there. To let her explore it while he took care of her.

He absolutely loved it.

"Charlie," he whispered as he put his hand on her back and gently rubbed it. "It's time to wake up."

She whined and buried her head into her pillow more.

"Come on, little one. You need to wake up, or you won't sleep tonight," Finn said.

"Nooo," she drawled out and tried to get away from his hand.

Finn gently picked her up out of the crib and held her against him. He slowly started to rub her back and rock her at the same time.

"Come on, little cupcake. It's time to wake up."

She nestled her head into his shoulder, but he was quick to move her so she couldn't. He didn't want her to fall back asleep since she still had to sleep tonight. Finn also wanted to talk to her about fully moving in, and he needed her fully awake for that.

"Cupcake, I need you to wake up so that we can have a discussion."

Charlotte blinked her eyes open and looked up at Finn. He could tell that she was still tired, but he knew that if he let her sleep anymore, she wouldn't fall asleep again. He wanted her beauty sleep, but he also wanted Charlotte to sleep through the night.

She needed all the sleep she could get since she had to wake up so early and work. Finn didn't realize how close of an eye he was going to have to keep on Charlotte, but after she spent a couple days with him, he knew.

Health wasn't a huge priority for her, but it was for him. He wanted her to be at her best, to be the best version of herself, and he was determined. He wanted her to be healthy and thriving in life.

"Daddy?" Charlotte whispered.

Finn smiled at her and gently set her on the ground. He held on to her waist in case she felt dizzy or her legs gave out. She had just woken up, and he didn't want her to get hurt.

"Daddy has some food, and then we can talk," he said.

Charlotte grabbed his hand, and Finn let her out of the nursery and to the kitchen. He had a little snack for her already on the kitchen counter. Apples and peanut butter because that was her new favorite thing right now, and it was healthy. Finn didn't think that she would like it so much but was super happy when she did.

"What do we need to talk about?" Charlotte asked as Finn helped her onto a chair.

For the past several days, Charlotte had liked to eat on Finn's lap, but right now, he needed her to focus while they had this conversation. He didn't want her to not hear something he said because she got turned on.

"Eat this, and I'll tell you," he said.

Finn waited for Charlotte to take a couple bites of her apples and peanut butter before he started to talk. He wanted to make sure that she was actually going to eat because he had a feeling once he said what they were going to talk about that she wasn't going to want to talk anymore.

He watched as she took several more bites.

"Such a good girl for Daddy."

Charlotte beamed up at him when he said that, and he couldn't help but smile. She was a good girl when she wanted to be, but when she wanted to be naughty, she was naughty. Charlotte had landed herself several spankings for putting herself in danger, not following his rules, and throwing temper tantrums.

Finn didn't necessarily like punishing her, but he knew that when she disobeyed, he was going to give her a punishment. She needed to learn that if she acted out, there were going to be consequences.

He wanted her to know that somebody cared for her, and that's why he had these rules. He didn't just have rules to spank her when she disobeyed. He made these rules so that she was safe, she felt loved, and knew that somebody was there to look out for her. Sometimes Finn got a vibe that not many people looked out for Charlotte's and he wanted to be there for her.

He wanted to be there for her because he loved her.

Finn's whole body froze at that thought. He loved her and there's no doubt about it. Was it too soon to tell Charlotte that he loved her?

He didn't want to scare her, but he also didn't want to wait a long time and it be too late.

"What did you want to talk about, Daddy?" Charlotte asked as she took another bite of her apples and peanut butter.

Finn stood in front of her behind the counter, and he looked at her for a second. She was so precious, and he was lucky to have her as his little girl, his little cupcake. She made him feel extremely lucky and blessed to have her in his life.

"Move in with me," Finn said.

He thought about sugarcoating it and explaining everything, but he didn't think that was the wisest thing right now. He didn't want to give her mixed signals or confuse her when he was trying to explain it.

"I love you, and I want you to fully move in with me. You spent several days at my house, and it feels alive when you're here. It feels like home for the first time."

The apple fell from Charlotte's hand as she stared at him in shock.

"I know I just dropped a bombshell of information, but I needed you to know. I love you, and I want to spend the rest of my life with you. I want to wake up and have you in my arms, put you down for naps during the day, make sweet long love to you at night and during the day. I want you all to myself because I don't share."

Her mouth hung open as Finn continued to talk. He wanted to lay everything out there so that when she made her decision, she knew everything. Finn didn't want told anything back because it was about time that he told her everything.

"I want to spoil you rotten until we get old. I want to love you unconditionally the rest of our lives. I want you to move into my house because without you, it doesn't feel like home, it feels like an empty house," Finn continued to speak. "Before I met you, I never wanted to come home because it was empty. I worked long hours so that I had an excuse not to come home. Then I saw you lying on the floor of the club, coloring, and I knew that you were mine. I knew that you were it for me, and I was right because when I brought you here when you were sick, it instantly felt like a home. It didn't feel empty and cold but alive."

Tears had started to stream down Charlotte's face, and Finn wanted to wrap her up in his arms, but he needed to get everything out. He needed her to hear everything he said before he hugged her, kissed her.

"I know we've only known each other for a couple of months, but it feels so right. My dad used to say that you'll know when you know. And I know that you're the one for me."

Finn leaned forward and kissed her forehead. He could tell that he was starting to overwhelm her, but he needed to get this out so that she could think over it. Finn wasn't going to require an answer tonight because he knew that she needed time to think about it.

It was a big step, and he didn't want to rush her into anything. Yes, he did want her to move in with him as soon as possible, but he wanted her to move in because she wanted to, not because he wanted it.

It was a delicate balance because Finn knew that sometimes Charlotte wanted to please him. And while he loved that, he also didn't want to force her into anything.

"You can have time to think about it because I don't want to rush you into anything. I just wanted to let you know how I'm feeling toward you. I didn't want to keep that I love you to myself anymore or that I want you to move in with me."

Charlotte nodded her head, and Finn wiped away the tears on her cheeks.

"I-I don't know what to say," Charlotte whispered.

"It's okay not to say anything. I don't expect you to give

me an answer right now or know what to say. It's a lot." Finn walked around the counter and sat right next to her.

Charlotte got off of her seat and climbed into his lap. He felt a little relief that she didn't just leave the house because she was overwhelmed or go to her room, but she decided to sit in his lap.

It was a good sign, or, well, he hoped it was a good sign.

"Daddy," Charlotte said as she snuggled into his body.

Finn wrapped his arms around her body and held her close to him. He loved that she fit next to his body so well. It felt so right to have her in his arms, and he enjoyed every second of it.

They sat in each other's embrace for a while, just enjoying being together. Finn wanted this for the rest of his life. He could envision them sitting on the back porch, Charlotte on his lap as they rocked and relaxed.

That's what he wanted, that's what he'd always wanted. He didn't know that a year ago, but when he laid eyes on Charlotte, he immediately knew that was what he'd always craved, always wanted.

"Daddy. I love you too. I think I've loved you for a little while," Charlotte whispered.

Finn's heart skipped a beat, and he couldn't help the smile that spread across his face. His little cupcake loved him back.

"I don't know about moving in with you yet. I need to think about that. It's a...it's a big step," she whispered and buried her head into his chest.

"That's okay, little cupcake."

Charlotte moved her body around, so her chest was pressed up against his chest, and her legs were on either side of his hips. Finn loved that she was comfortable enough to do that because when they first got together, she wasn't.

Finn held her close and rubbed up and down her back. He wanted to spend the next couple minutes just holding her and enjoying that they both love each other.

Charlotte loved him.

It was hard to wrap his brain around that for a second because he never thought he would find a little girl that would love him. Finn thought that he would be alone forever and die alone.

But Charlotte proved him wrong. He knew that she was his the moment he laid eyes on her, but he had to wait for her to reciprocate the feelings. And he was glad that he waited because right now, holding her and knowing that she loved him was the best thing ever.

Charlotte started to wiggle, and Finn let out a groan. He could feel himself starting to get hard, and he knew if she didn't stop soon, he was going to have his way with her.

"Charlotte, you need to stop," Finn groaned.

She continued to wiggle and grind herself against him.

"I don't want to, Daddy," she whispered in his ear. "I want you."

Finn's head rolled back, and he closed his eyes tight. He needed all the strength he could muster up to not take her to his room and have his way with her.

"Charlotte, I need you to know that once I have a taste of you, you won't ever be able to leave. You'll be mine," Finn said as he looked at her.

"I know, Daddy. I want you."

That was all it took for Finn to be convinced that she

wanted to be with him for the rest of their lives. Finn stood up with Charlotte in his arms and walked toward his room.

He walked in and threw her onto the bed. He stalked slowly toward her as he unbuttoned his shirt.

"Last chance, little cupcake. Are you sure?" he asked.

"Take me, Daddy."

CHAPTER THIRTY

CHARLOTTE

*C*harlotte stared at her Daddy as he walked the rest of the way to her. Nerves filled her body as he pulled off his shirt and tossed it to the side.

His chest and torso were chiseled with muscles. Charlotte's mouth went dry as she looked over his chest at his tattoos. She was a sucker for tattoos, and he had several.

How did she miss them?

They littered the upper part of his chest and arms. In big bold lettering were the numbers nineteen-eighty-three. Was that the year he was born?

Charlotte knew that he was on the older side, and knowing he was forty turned her on even more.

A shiny object caught her attention, and she found herself looking at his right nipple that was pierced. How would it feel to have her tongue graze across it as she made her way down to his cock?

"Little cupcake, if you keep looking at me like I'm some meal, I won't last long." Daddy's voice brought her out of her thoughts.

Charlotte looked in his eyes and gave him a shy smile. He looked absolutely delicious, and Charlotte couldn't wait to get a taste of him.

Daddy got onto the bed and cupped her face with his hands. He leaned forward and gently brushed his lips against hers, a small whimper coming out of her mouth.

His soft lips guided Charlotte's as he gently pushed her body down onto the bed. Charlotte's legs fell open, and Daddy's body went in between them.

"Such a good girl," he said against her lips.

His hips met hers, and he ground his erection against her. A soft moan slipped through her mouth, and her back arched.

"Please," she whimpered. "Please."

Daddy's lips trailed down her neck but stopped where her jaw and neck met and sucked on it. Shivers passed through Charlotte's body as pleasure coursed through her.

Kisses started to trail down her neck but stopped when her shirt got in the way.

"This needs to go," he growled.

Daddy grabbed the bottom of Charlotte's shirt and yanked it above her head as she brought her body off the mattress.

She had completely forgotten that when she took a nap, all she was in was her Daddy's shirt. She didn't have a bra or underwear on underneath. Charlotte's hands closed against her naked chest to cover up her boobs. She wasn't small, but she wasn't big either.

"Stop!" Daddy called out.

Charlotte stared at him with wide eyes, her hands still covering her boobs.

"Hands to the side," he commanded.

She slowly brought her hands away from her boobs and laid them on the bed, grabbing a fistful of the sheets as nerves filled her body.

Charlotte felt the heat of her Daddy's stare on her body, and a shiver ran through her. She tried to close her legs, but his body stopped her.

"So beautiful," he whispered as he trailed kisses down her neck and toward her boobs.

Sucking one boob into his mouth, he started to swirl his tongue around her nipple and nipped at the skin.

"Ohhhhhh." Charlotte's back arched as his teeth grazed across her nipple.

Everything felt so good, like she was floating on a cloud.

"Do you like it when Daddy sucks on your pretty little nipples?" he asked as he moved over t the other one.

Charlotte nodded her head, but when she didn't verbally answer, he bit down on her nipple.

"Words," he murmured against her skin as he looked up at her, still sucking on her nipple.

"Yes, Daddy," she moaned.

His fingers lightly trailed down her body, leaving goose-bumps and pleasure. Her breathing got faster as he moved his fingers to her pussy and cupped it.

"This is mine," he huskily said. "All mine."

Charlotte nodded her head in agreement. "Yours, Daddy."

She moved her hips up, trying to create some friction to bring her pleasure.

"Not so fast. Daddy wants to appreciate your body," he said as he pushed her hips back down.

A soft whine escaped past her lips, but with a smack to her pussy, it quieted it down. Pleasure coursed through her body as he slapped her pussy again.

"Please," she begged.

His fingers slid through her folds, coating them with her juices.

"So wet for Daddy."

Sliding two fingers into her, he slowly pumped it in and out. Charlotte felt like she was on cloud nine as he continued to pump his fingers into her and rub her clit.

Pressure started to build inside of her, and she knew she was close to coming.

"Daddy!" Her voice got higher. "Please let me come."

"Not yet, little cupcake. I want my cock inside of you when you come."

Charlotte closed her eyes and gripped the sheets tighter. She willed everything inside of her not to come right then and there.

Daddy pulled his fingers out of her, and she whined at the loss of contact. She still felt the buzz from his fingers inside of her.

His belt jingling caught her attention, and she looked at him as he dropped his pants and underwear to the floor. Her jaw dropped at how big he was. She had no doubt that he was going to make himself fit inside of her, it was just a matter of how long it took and if both of them could wait that long.

"Are you on birth control?" he asked Charlotte.

"Yes, Daddy," she whispered.

She had been on it for a while to help with her periods since they were brutal.

Charlotte stopped Daddy when he went to go grab a condom.

"No condom," she said.

"Are you sure?" he asked.

"Yes. I'm clean."

"I'm clean too."

He got back on the bed and in between her legs.

"Be a good girl for Daddy, and take his cock," he said as he aligned his dick at her entrance.

Taking a deep breath, Charlotte looked at him and nodded her head. She was so ready for him, and he was taking his sweet time.

"I want to fill this pussy with my seed. Breed you until you beg me to stop," he said as he pushed himself inside of her.

A small scream bubbled up out of her throat and into the room. Full. That's all she felt as he filled her with his cock.

Daddy pulled back before ramming into her again. Charlotte's walls clenched around his cock, and her back arched even more.

"P-please," she moaned as he continued to fuck her.

"Wait for me," he commanded.

His fingers rubbed her clit in a circular motion, and her hips bucked up to try and meet his thrusts. The pressure and pleasure coursing through her body was getting closer, and she knew she wasn't going to last much longer.

"Daddy," she moaned. "I need to come."

He groaned and sped up his thrusts. "You wait for Daddy."

Charlotte's toes curled into the bed, and her walls

clenched around him. His thrusts came faster, and she knew he was close as well.

"Come for Daddy," he commanded as he pinched her clit and thrust into her.

Charlotte screamed as she let go and came around his cock. Her walls tightened even more, sending him over the edge.

Daddy's cum filled her as she came down from her release. Charlotte felt him gently pull out and get off the bed. She watched him as he went into the bathroom, but she didn't make any move to get up. She didn't have it in her.

Washcloth in hand, her Daddy came back into the room and gently started to clean Charlotte up.

"Ooooo." She relaxed as the warm washcloth glided across her pussy.

"Such a good girl," he praised her.

Daddy threw the washcloth in the dirty hamper before he picked Charlotte up, walked to the bathroom, and sat her down on the toilet.

"Pee." He stood back and watched her.

Charlotte's cheeks turned bright red, and she looked down.

"I've got a shy bladder," she whispered. "You can leave."

"Nope. There's nothing between a little and her Daddy. You can pee in front of me," he replied. "I'll turn the water on so I can't hear."

Charlotte waited for the water to turn on before she started to go to the bathroom. She knew it was important to pee after she had sex, but she didn't know how she felt about peeing in front of him. Charlotte quickly wiped herself and looked over at her Daddy.

"Such a good girl for Daddy," he said as he picked her up.

He walked back into the room and laid her down on the bed.

"Do you want Moody?" he asked.

Charlotte immediately nodded her head and snuggled into the pillow. Daddy walked out of the room, and when he came back, he had Moody in his hands.

Charlotte made grabby hands, and her Daddy gave her stuffie to her. She snuggled up to it and felt him get into bed and wrap his arms around her.

"Good night, my little cupcake," he whispered in her ear.

"Good night, Daddy."

CHAPTER THIRTY-ONE

CHARLOTTE

$\mathcal{D}$addy had asked Charlotte the other day if she would move in with him. Well, he had said a whole lot of things that overwhelmed Charlotte.

He poured his heart out to her, and all she could say back was that she also loved him. It was true; she loved him with her whole heart.

Everything about him was perfect. Yes, he did give spankings and timeouts in the corner, but she knew in the end that he was doing it out of love. He wanted her to be better, happy, and healthy, and that warmed her heart.

Not many people had wanted that for her when she was growing up. They didn't care if she ate enough, slept enough, or was happy. They just cared about themselves, but Daddy didn't. He cared about her and wanted her to thrive in life.

Charlotte had thought long and hard about moving in with him. She didn't know if she should because what if they broke up? Where would she go then?

Even if they didn't break up, would she have her own space to relax? She hadn't shared a house with anyone in a long time, and she was worried that moving in with him wouldn't end well.

What if they got sick of each other when she moved in?

Charlotte had stayed the past two nights, and it was amazing, but that was just two nights. Moving in with him would be for the rest of their lives or until they got sick of each other.

She didn't want to have to think about all of this, but she needed to. She needed to give him an answer because it wasn't fair to leave him hanging. He had poured his heart out to her and asked her to move in.

Charlotte was sort of already living with him, but most of her stuff was over at her house. She had several pairs of clothes here, and Daddy had bought her some more, but her stuff was still at her house waiting for her.

Tears of frustration filled Charlotte's eyes. She just wished it would be an easy decision and that all these bad thoughts wouldn't come to mind, but she couldn't help it. Charlotte had always needed to think about the good and the bad when she decided things.

She had been on her own for so long that she had to. If she didn't, then sometimes there were consequences that she had to deal with.

Charlotte wiped away the tears and sucked in several deep breaths. Maybe it was wise for her to say she couldn't move in to be safe. Or tell Daddy that she could but keep her house and the stuff in it, so in case of anything, she could just move back in there.

Just the thought of telling him that she couldn't move broke her heart. She wanted so badly to move in with him, but she was worried. Who wouldn't be worried in this situation?

She had been independent for so long, and she was worried that when she moved in, she wouldn't have that independence anymore.

Charlotte knew that her independence was important. She loved relying on her Daddy, but it was just knowing that she had a place to go if she needed to ease her.

Would she have a place like that if she moved in?

Charlotte knew that their dynamic was twenty-four seven. That's what they had agreed on, and she loved it, but everybody needed their own space at some point.

She didn't know how to convey that to her Daddy without hurting his feelings. That was the last thing she wanted to do.

She knew communication was important, and she was going to talk to him at some point about this. She just didn't know when.

Should she do it right now, or should she wait? Charlotte worried that if she waited, it wouldn't go well, but she also worried that if she said it now, it also wouldn't go well.

"Have you told the cafe that you won't be working any more?" Daddy asked as he sat down next to her.

Charlotte crawled into his lap and placed her head on his chest. She loved times like this when they could just sit together and relax.

Today was Charlotte's day off from the bakery, and they hadn't done much, but that was okay with her. She loved spending time with him and couldn't wait to do it every day when she got home from work.

"I told them four days ago that I wouldn't be working there anymore. They told me it was okay," she whispered.

She hoped he couldn't tell that she was about to cry. He would worry and tell her that she could talk to him about anything, and she didn't know how to talk about it without hurting his feelings.

"Little cupcake, what's wrong?" he asked.

Charlotte buried her head into his chest and started to cry.

"Oh, cupcake. It's okay."

His hands wrapped around her and held her close to him.

"Let it all out. You're okay."

Charlotte continued to cry into his chest.

"Can you tell Daddy what's wrong?" he asked.

She shook her head. She didn't want to hurt his feelings.

"Can you listen to Daddy?"

"Yes," she whispered.

"I have a feeling I know why you're crying, and I want you to listen to everything I have to say."

Charlotte grabbed his shirt with her hand and relaxed into his embrace. Tears were still streaming down her face, but she was paying attention to him.

"I bet it's about me asking you to move in with me. I want you to know that whatever you decide, I'll support you. If you don't want to move in, then I won't force you to, and if you do, then I'll help you move in."

Charlotte sucked in a breath after a sob escaped past her mouth. How did he know what she was thinking about?

"I bet you've been on your own for a while and you're

scared if you move in that you won't have your own space or it won't work out. I want you to know that if you do move in, you don't need to be afraid. You'll have your room for your little that you can go be in by yourself. You can tell Daddy when you need that alone time, and Daddy will leave you alone."

Charlotte let out a breath of air and relaxed more into his embrace. It was like he could read her mind.

She was glad at this moment that he could because she knew what he thought about it. He was reassuring her that it was okay.

"You can come to Daddy for anything. You can talk to me about anything. Your worries, what you're scared of anything. Daddy also understands that you may not have wanted to come because you didn't want to hurt my feelings. I want you to know that you can tell me anything, and you won't hurt my feelings. I want you to be honest."

Charlotte nodded her head against his chest. She knew now that she could come to him for anything to speak her mind.

"I'm sorry," she whispered.

"What are you sorry for?" Daddy asked.

Charlotte took a deep breath in and tightened her fist around his shirt. She wanted the comfort right now as she spoke to him.

"I'm sorry for not coming to you and saying this. I was worried that your feelings would get hurt. I didn't know how to bring this up, but I promised that I was going to. You just beat me to it."

"I forgive you, my little cupcake. I knew you were going to come to me eventually about it, but I wanted to ease your worries."

Charlotte moved her head and looked up at him, but her hand was still tightly gripping his shirt.

"How did you know?"

"Daddies always know. But if you really wanna know, your body language and your facial expressions told me. I knew after I spilled my guts to you that it was gonna worry you. I've seen it happen before with my friend. His little one has been independent since she was a tiny little girl, and moving in with him was hard because she didn't know if she would have her own space. I saw it firsthand, and I knew I needed to address it with you."

Tears welled up in her eyes. "Thank you for being such a good Daddy."

He held her tightly against him and ran his hand up and down her back.

"So what's your decision?" Daddy asked.

"I'll move in," she whispered. "I-I don't wanna get rid of my house though. I just...I just think I can do good with it."

"What were you thinking?"

"I don't know. Maybe renting it out? I honestly haven't given it much thought, but I know that I don't want to sell it."

"I think that's a good idea. We can brainstorm ideas together. If you want."

Charlotte beamed up at him. "I love that idea."

"Great! We'll start writing ideas down on a piece of paper."

Charlotte snuggled up into his arms and relaxed.

"Thank you, Daddy."

"You're welcome."

They sat there for several minutes, basking in each other's embrace. Charlotte felt so much more at ease knowing if she needed space that she could have it. She didn't realize how much she had worried about that until he mentioned it.

"Want to go eat ice cream? I've got some in the freezer," Daddy suggested.

"What flavor?"

Charlotte knew there was only one right type of ice cream flavor.

"Cookies and cream, vanilla, chocolate, and butter pecan."

Her stomach rumbled at the mention of cookies and cream ice cream. It was so delicious, and she could eat her weight in it.

"Cookies and cream!" she screamed and scrambled off of his lap.

Charlotte raced out of the room and toward the kitchen.

"No running!" Daddy yelled after her, but she didn't pay any attention.

She wanted the ice cream right now.

"Charlotte Ann! You stop running right this instant, or your bottom will be bright red!"

That didn't stop Charlotte from running into the kitchen. Nothing was going to stop her from getting her ice cream.

A hand wrapped around her waist and picked her up. Several hard swats landed on her bottom, making her yell in pain.

"Stop!" she screamed. "Stoooooop."

"In the corner right now," Daddy said and placed her feet back on the ground.

"No!" she stomped her foot and looked up at him.

CHAPTER THIRTY-TWO

CHARLOTTE

"*No?*" Daddy said. "I'm going to count to three, and if you aren't in the corner by three, there will be more consequences."

Charlotte stood her ground. He had no right to swat her bottom and tell her to go into the corner. She didn't do anything wrong.

"One."

She didn't move from her spot.

"Two."

Maybe she should move because he seemed very serious about this.

"Three. That's it." Daddy grabbed onto her arm and guided her over to the corner. "Nose touching right here and bottom sticking out."

Charlotte turned around and crossed her arms, glaring at her Daddy. She didn't understand what she was getting in trouble for. Running wasn't bad, and she didn't break the rule of her being in danger.

"Nose in the corner," he said again as he turned her around.

"I don't wanna!" Charlotte yelled and turned around once again. "I didn't do anything wrong!"

Daddy let out a sigh and kneeled down onto the ground. He grabbed her face in between his hands and looked her in the eye.

"Daddy told you not to run, and I expect you to obey that. You could've slipped and fallen on your head. Or you could've ran into a wall or glass door and cut yourself," he explained. "Daddy just wants you to be safe, and running in the house is dangerous."

"It's not dangerous!" She stomped her foot. "I just wanted ice cream!"

How could running be that dangerous? Yes, she could slip and fall, but it wouldn't hurt that bad, would it?

"Charlotte, it is dangerous. You could be running and slipping which could result in cracking your head open. There are a lot of corners in our house, and you could hit your head on one of them and need surgery," he explained.

Charlotte's face paled at the mention of cracking her head open and surgery. She didn't realize that those could happen if she ran in the house.

"I'm sorry, Daddy," she whispered and closed her eyes.

All she wanted was ice cream, and she had thrown all caution out the door to get it.

"I know you are, but you disobeyed and then threw a tantrum when I tried to punish you and explain the reasoning behind it," Daddy said. "Let Daddy take your pants and underwear off, and then you go into the corner."

Charlotte hung her head as her Daddy started to pull her

pants and underwear down. She knew he only wanted to keep her safe, and she ignored it.

"Corner in the nose and your bottom out. I'll start the time once it's done," he said and patted her bottom lightly.

She scurried to the corner and tucked her nose in and her bottom out. She was on display in the corner, and she didn't like that one bit. Charlotte pulled her shirt down to try and cover her bottom, but Daddy lightly tapped her hand.

"No covering your bottom," he said. "I'll be right back. Don't move."

Charlotte stood in the corner and thought about what she did. She couldn't believe that she talked back to him and threw a tantrum. Charlotte didn't know why she did that.

"Daddy's going to put ginger in your bottom as you stand in the corner," he said.

She kept her mouth shut and didn't say anything. Why was he putting ginger in her bottom?

Daddy pulled her cheeks apart and circled her anus with his finger. She squirmed and tried to pull away, but a quick swat to the bottom stopped her.

His finger gently pushed into her and moved around some. Charlotte didn't like it, but she started to feel herself getting turned on.

"Take a deep breath in," Daddy instructed, and Charlotte followed suit. "Now blow it out."

Charlotte felt something wider than her Daddy's finger insert into her bottom, the ginger. She relaxed when he let go of her cheeks. That wasn't so bad. It was uncomfortable a little because something was halfway inside of her, but it didn't feel bad at all.

That's what Charlotte thought in the beginning, but then

all of the sudden she started to feel a burning sensation in her anus. The discomfort and burning continued to grow as she stood in the corner.

"Daddy!" She raised her voice. "It burns. Take it out!"

"It's supposed to burn. It's part of your punishment," daddy replied.

Charlotte wiggled, but it only made the burning sensation worse. Tears streamed down her face as the burning intensified.

"Stay still," he commanded.

She tried her hardest, but it was so difficulty. How much longer did she have to stand in this corner for? It felt like she had been here for hours and hours, but she knew it had only been a couple of minutes.

Charlotte sniffled and tried to hold in her tears, but she was unsuccessful. She never wanted to disobey her Daddy ever again. if this was the type of punishment she was going to get. She was going to try and be the best girl ever.

Daddy's hand touched her back, and she flinched.

"It's okay," daddy said and kept his hand on her lower back. "I'm just going to take out the ginger."

Charlotte held her breath as he spread her butt cheeks and took a hold of the ginger. He twisted it, pulled it out and pushed it back in several times.

A sob escaped past her lips as the burning was unbearable. When was he going to take it out?

Daddy pushed it in super far before he slowly started to take it out. Charlotte thought that the burning sensation would go away when it was out of her bottom, but it still continued to burn.

"You can turn around now," Daddy said.

She turned around, her face tear stricken. She so badly wanted to just run into his arms and have him hold her, but she didn't know if she was allowed to move. She didn't want to add on to her punishment.

"Do you know what you did wrong?" he asked.

"I continued to wun when you told me not to," Charlotte whispered.

"That's right, little cupcake. Do you know why I asked you not to run?"

"It's dangerous, and I could have huwt myself."

"That's right," Daddy said as he got onto his knees and opened his arms. "Come here."

Charlotte launched herself into his arms and cried when his arms wrapped around her. She felt so bad that she disobeyed because she didn't want to, but she did. The want for ice cream overcame her logic, and at that moment she didn't care what she did, the only goal was to get the ice cream.

"It's okay. All is forgiven now," he murmured in her ear.

Daddy stood up with Charlotte in his arms and walked over to the couch. He sat down and held Charlotte close to him. She loved the feeling of his arms around her and could never get enough of it.

"You know I just want to keep you safe and healthy, right? I only have the best interests for you," Daddy said as he slowly rocked them back and forth.

Charlotte nodded her head because she knew that. He had explained it several times that he just wanted what was best for her, even if she didn't know it was good for her at the time. It was hard, but she trusted him with that.

"I love you, little cupcake." He kissed the top of her head.

Daddy moved Charlotte around, so her head was on his arm and leaning to his chest. She relaxed in his embrace and cherished being held like this. He moved his arm to the side to grab something, but she didn't know what it was.

"Open up," he encouraged her.

Charlotte opened her mouth, and he slipped the nipple in.

"Such a good girl," Daddy said as she started to drink the protein shake in the bottle.

This was one of Charlotte's favorite times. To be held in his arms and be fed with a bottle. It always made her feel small but also loved because her Daddy took the time to sit and feed her.

"Sometimes you're going to be naughty, and that's okay, but you're never a bad person. I want to address this so down the road you don't get confused by that or think you're a bad person because you were naughty," Daddy started as Charlotte continued to drink. "Daddy is here to help guide you, make you feel safe, cherished, and loved."

Charlotte sucked on the nipple faster as he explained everything. She had started to feel like she was a bad person after her punishment.

She relaxed in his embrace as her Daddy shook the bottle a little.

"Finish all of this up, and then Daddy will put you down for a nap."

Charlotte whined at the thought of taking a nap right now. She didn't want to leave his arms, and she didn't want to go to sleep.

"No whining. You're tired, and it's nap time. Afterwards, we can do something fun together."

Charlotte finished her bottle, and Daddy put a pacifier in her mouth and rocked her until she fell asleep.

EPILOGUE

CHARLOTTE

*I*t had been several weeks since the ginger was put in her bottom. Did that keep her out of trouble? No, but Charlotte hadn't been as naughty or talked back as much.

She had found her footing and was comfortable enough to be a little naughty sometimes. She had been comfortable before, but knowing that she hadn't fully moved in and that he could kick her out worried her. Daddy could still kick her out, but he had told her that she was the one for him, and nothing was going to change that.

After that tragic day, her Daddy had made plans to get all of her things from the house and bring them to his. Well, their house now.

Daddy encouraged Charlotte to think of it as her house as well because it was now. She was still getting used to calling it to their house, her house, her home, but it was growing on her, and she felt giddy every time she said it.

Her Daddy had Michael, Marco, and Jackson help bring her stuff from her house to their house. None of them would let her lift a single thing, and it kind of annoyed her, but at the same time, she was happy she didn't have to carry all the heavy things.

It had been a pain in the butt to move everything when she initially moved into her house, and she didn't want to have to do that over again. Charlotte tried to carry her stuffies or coloring books in, but daddy told her that she should just relax on the couch and watch some TV.

And so that was what she did while they brought everything in. She would giggle when all four of them made faces at her as they walked in.

"Little cupcake! Where are you hiding?"

Charlotte giggled but quickly quieted down. She didn't want her Daddy to find her right now. They were playing a game of hide and seek, and she wanted to win. Charlotte was the best at playing this game and always found the best hiding spots that no one thought of.

Maybe her Daddy would ever find her, and she'd win. Fear coursed through her body with the thought of Daddy never finding her. She didn't want that to happen.

"Where are you, my little cupcake?" Daddy called out.

Tears welled up in her eyes, and she burst through the closet doors.

"Daddy! I'm right here!" Her voice held panic, and she started to run toward the door to the room.

Arms wrapped around her midsection and held her close.

"What's wrong?" Daddy asked.

By now, the tears had started to run down her face. "I-I t-thought," Charlotte sobbed and couldn't finish her sentence.

Daddy sat on the ground and held her close to him. "It's okay, cupcake. Take a couple deep breaths for me."

He placed a hand on her chest and slowly breathed in to help ground her.

"Such a good girl," he whispered in her ear. "Now, what gave you a fright?"

Charlotte took a deep breath in and felt the fear course through her again. She always wanted her Daddy to find her when they played.

"I t-thought you wouldn't ever find me!"

Daddy held her tighter against him. "Not possible. Daddy will always find you. You're Daddy's little cupcake."

Charlotte snuggled into his embrace and relaxed. She had worried he wouldn't find her, and then she would be lost for forever.

The shrill of a phone ringing broke up their moment. Daddy quickly answered it and walked away. Charlotte knew that it was one of the wonders of the club. He normally never walked away from her unless it was one of the other owners.

Daddy never kept anything from her, but club business was his business and not hers. Charlotte didn't mind because she knew she would get bored with all the admin stuff. She didn't envy her Daddy in that regard.

Charlotte was happy to bake and come home to her Daddy or go to the club and sit in his office or play with other littles, like Janie.

Janie and Charlotte had gotten pretty close over the past few days. She was there more and more, and Charlotte saw Mac watching from a distance sometimes. Charlotte knew something was up the day Janie and her had met. The way

Janie wouldn't look at Mac in the eyes and had to leave once he got there.

Something was definitely up, and Charlotte was going to ask Janie the next time she saw her. She wanted to help her friend find a Daddy, and from what Charlotte had seen from Mac, he was perfect for her. Or, well, she thought he was perfect for Janie.

"Little cupcake?" Daddy called out.

Charlotte turned around and beamed up at her Daddy.

"Can I borrow some of your things? Clothes, bottle, diapers, and maybe a stuffie?" he asked.

What could he possibly want with her stuff? Why would he need to borrow it?

"There's a little girl that Michael found who needs some things urgently. If you don't want to let him borrow some of your things, we could go shopping together for some of the stuff she needs."

Thoughts swirled through her mind. What could the little possibly need so urgently?

"She's been hurt. I can't say much more than that, but she doesn't want to leave the house right now," Daddy explained. "We wouldn't be able to see her cause we don't want to scare her anymore than she already is."

"She can borrow my things," Charlotte whispered.

"Thank you." Daddy kissed the top of her head.

Charlotte watched as her Daddy started to get some things together and put them in a bag. She got up from her spot and walked over to him.

How could the little have gotten hurt? Who would hurt her? Why would someone hurt her?

"It's okay, little cupcake. The girl is healing now. She's in

279

good hands with Michael. He'll take care of her." Her Daddy ran his hands through her hair.

"Otay," she whispered, not feeling so sure about that.

She worried about her, and she didn't even meet the girl yet. Would she ever meet the girl?

"I'm going to have Mac pick up this stuff and give it to Michael," Daddy said.

"Why?" Charlotte looked up at him.

"Because my little cupcake needs me right now. I can see the worry on your face. We're going to snuggle and relax together."

Charlotte nodded her head and watched as he put the bag outside the front door and picked her up.

"My good little cupcake," he whispered in her ear. "Such a good girl."

Charlotte blushed and buried her head into his shoulder.

"I'm so glad you walked into my club that night."

She relaxed in his arms. "I'm glad you came down to talk to me."

"I love you."

"I love you too."

KEEP UP WITH EVERLY!

Sign up for my newsletter to get teasers, cover reveals, updates, and extra content!

Everly Raine Newsletter

SCAN ME TO SIGN UP NOW!

Get a free short story when you do!

ACKNOWLEDGMENTS

There are so many people I want to thank.

Thank you to L.G. Knight for helping me through the whole process! You have helped me so much and I'm so thankful that you took the time to answer all my (many) questions.

Thank you to all the beta readers for taking your time to read my rough draft and point out things that needed to change, things that needed to be clarified more, and overall everything.

Thank you to my ARC readers for taking the time and chance on me as a new author!

I really appreciate everyone I mentioned and didn't mention. Thank you to everyone who has taken the time to read this book.

ABOUT THE AUTHOR

Everly Raine is an emerging author of age play books. Want to follow along in her journey as an author?

FB Group: https://www.facebook.com/groups/878978066732860/

IG: https://www.instagram.com/authoreverlyraine/

Goodreads: https://www.goodreads.com/author/show/30503603.Everly_Raine

ALSO BY EVERLY RAINE

Missouri Daddies

Daddy's Little Cupcake

Daddy's Little Survivor (Coming Summer 2023)

Made in the USA
Columbia, SC
12 August 2024

39865399R00163